His shadow lay over the rocks as he bent, ending. Why not endless till the farthest star? Darkly they are there behind this light, darkness shining in the brightness, delta of Cassiopeia, worlds. Me sits there with his augur's rod of ash, in borrowed sandals, by day beside a livid sea, unbeheld, in violet night walking beneath a reign of uncouth stars. I throw this ended shadow from me, manshape ineluctable, call it back. Endless, would it be mine, form of my form? Who watches me here? Who ever anywhere will read these written words?

—JAMES JOYCE: *Ulysses*

MANSHAPE

John Brunner

DAW BOOKS, INC.
DONALD A. WOLLHEIM, PUBLISHER
1633 Broadway, New York, NY 10019

Printing history

This novel is based on a novella entitled BRIDGE TO AZRAEL which appeared in *Amazing Stories* February 1964 copyright © 1963 by Ziff-Davis Publishing Company. Under the title ENDLESS SHADOW the same text was published as half of Ace Doublebook F-299 copyright © 1964 by John Brunner (copyright assigned 1966 to Brunner Fact & Fiction Limited); the rights in the latter edition reverted to the author in 1971.

The present text has been wholly revised and expanded to about 150% of the length of the former novella.

The epigraph from *Ulysses* by James Joyce is by permission of Random House Inc., and copyright 1914, 1918, 1942, 1946, by Nora Joseph Joyce.

FIRST PRINTING, SEPTEMBER 1982

1 2 3 4 5 6 7 8 9

 DAW TRADEMARK REGISTERED
U.S. PAT. OFF. MARCA
REGISTRADA. HECHO EN U.S.A.

PRINTED IN U.S.A.

I

There are machines to move, that do move, half a million people a day from world to world as expeditiously as postal packages, and with them a million tons of freight like entries in a ledger, balancing.

And I am Jorgen Thorkild walking. On two legs in the ancient manner. Down a corridor that never feels the tread of human feet. Who can say how long since anybody came this way? There is of course no dust; that is seen to by efficient quiet machines, as and when necessary. The designer of the Bridge Centre worked in an age when our creations were not so totally reliable as now; he thought in terms of emergency exits, fire escapes, and the like.

Am I here because of an emergency? I guess I must be. But I wish sometimes I could find an emergency exit from my life. Saxena did.

But he must not think about Saxena. Determinedly he concentrated on the doors he was passing, hearing at the edge of audibility occasional voices and other noises. The building was in irregular interlocking layers. Some of it was underground, some had a view over the surrounding city, according to the taste of

5

the occupants. This layer was above ground. Not that one could have deduced the fact from this featureless grey corridor where sunlight had never shone since the day the roof was laid over it.

Signs said RIGER'S WORLD, and listed the names of that planet's Earthside representatives. What was he doing here? There was no need for him to come in person. He could have sent for any of them; simpler yet, he could have commanded a facsimile of himself to appear in their rooms, spoken as though they stood face to face without having moved. But here he was, and this door was named after Koriot Angoss.

Thorkild paused with his hand almost touching its lockplate. He was Director of the Bridge System. This, like any door in Bridge Centre, would open if he merely set his hand to it. Delaying, he listened.

Fined down to a sharp thin edge by insulation that took out all the bass frequencies: a man, singing. The dialect of Riger's World was not too far off Standard Earthside usage. The song was bawdy; it told of a drunken libertine whose liquor-lively tongue could seduce any woman, yet who failed to live up to her expectations when she yielded. After the first verse, someone with an instrument—it seemed acoustic rather than electronic—chorded in an accompaniment, feeling for the structure of the simple melody.

Thorkild closed the last gap between his hand and the door, and it swung wide.

Like every office in the building, this one was a replica of what might be found on its occupants' home planet; its modern equipment was disguised behind rough wooden panels, there were cured animal-skins on the floor, vases held locally-cultured flowers of curious green and golden shades. Even the smell of the air was—to the best of Thorkild's recollection—tolerably authentic. But the Bridge City loomed beyond the vast glass wall on its far side. It was as though one might look, and not merely travel, from this tired old Earth to its younger and more vigorous daughter-worlds.

Angoss was sitting on a padded, hand-crafted stool with a revolving top. He was an untidy man with wild hair and a grin that showed a gold incisor, gold being common where he came from. It was typical of him that he had retained the prosthetic rather than asking for a regenerated tooth, which on Earth could have been his free of charge. So too was his garb of coarse brown linen shirt and pants and red leather sandals. In one hand he held a mug of pale brown liquid, a kind of beer. On a long padded bench under the window sat his confidential human secretary, Maida Wenge, who was not so contemptuous of Earthside luxuries and wore a silky synthetic garment as smooth and elegant as Thorkild's own robe. On her lap reposed the instrument he had heard through the door; it was an air-bellows device, an accordion of sorts.

The song ended in surprise—more, Thorkild realised, at the interruption than because he had come through the door that was never used. Of course, on Riger's doors were still commonplace as a means of entry, and privacy not so highly valued.

Angoss walked himself around on the stool by making crabwise movements with his feet.

"Good day, Director!" he exclaimed, changing back from the dialect in which he had been singing to Standard Earthside. His accent showed slightly, but he had spent most of the past decade on Earth and worn it thin. Besides, the communication made possible by the Bridge System was once again pulling human speech back towards a common standard. He added, "Will you take a jar with us? The brewer is my cousin, and he sent me a barrel of his best as a year-day gift. I recommend!"

Thorkild shook his head, letting the door swing shut. He stood looking down at Angoss. It wasn't right. Was it? The way he acted could not possibly be fitting for a man in a post of such responsibility.

But he was unable to speak of right and wrong, fitting and unfitting, because he was unsure whether he was thinking of Angoss—or of himself.

Instead, he said, "You're sending us a problem, I understand."

Angoss got to his feet and helped himself to more beer from the barrel. It reposed on his desk, where one might rather have expected to see pictures and documents and tapes concerning work in hand. *Did* this man ever do anything that could properly be called work?

Blowing away an excess of foam, he said, "We don't have problems on Riger's. Do we?"

"One at least that you seem anxious to export." Thorkild spoke evenly, but that cost him effort. "The preacher—what's his name?"

"Oh, you must mean Rungley," Maida said, and Angoss gave a derisory snort as he resumed his stool.

"Oh, him! His sect is the Coppersnakes, isn't it? You can ignore them!" He drank with a slurping noise. "Are you sure you won't join us? This is first-rate!"

"I haven't time," Thorkild said. "And I came here for an answer, a proper answer."

Angoss parodied a look of hurt pride. "Don't you trust my evaluation? Aren't I supposed to be an expert?"

"It's all very well to say I can ignore him! But I don't like the sound of what he is, or what he does!"

"Director," Angoss said with a sigh, "how many crazy preachers have you known arrive by Bridge with the much publicised intention of converting Earth?"

"Scores! Hundreds, maybe! And a few have given trouble."

"Rungley won't be one of the few. Look: the Coppersnakes are an offshoot of a sect which once flourished in Continental North America, result of a bastard crossing between Christianity and an African fertility cult. They handle snakes as proof of faith. They have a built-in check-and-balance mechanism— every so often someone gets bitten and falls sick or dies, and half the congregation changes its collective mind. You slip a few king-cobras, kraits and mambas to Rungley, and inside a week he'll be in the hospital. Remember he's used to handling the domesticated snakes the sect took to Riger's. What you've got here on Earth must be a very different matter. Soon as he's made a fool of himself in public, he'll more than likely head for home."

It sounded like a sensible solution. Only . . . how to explain the haunting terror, the fear that this kind of mad foolhardiness was precisely the sort of thing that the population of weary old Earth might be looking for? In the far past there had been wars; even now there were fatal accidents; and as those grew fewer, there seemed to be more and ever more people in search of the stimulus that only gambling with death could give them—as though death alone could lend any sort of meaning to existence.

Moreover: sensible solutions from a man found in working hours (not long hours, not overly demanding work) boozing with his secretary and singing bawdy folksongs?

Thorkild found words at last. "What's their strength on Riger's?"

"They meet in a hand-carpentered wooden hut." Angoss took another pull at his beer. "Since Rungley announced he was coming to Earth, they've built an annexe to the church. They get maybe sixty to a meeting."

"Why the hell can't you keep your archaic survivals to yourself?" Thorkild snapped. He didn't mean to be so brusque, but he was raw-nerved, and not only from the Rungley problem. Reproachfully Maida looked at him with sombre, dark-pool eyes. She was beautiful by her own world's standards, but for Earthside tastes too broad in the hips; it had been centuries since giving easy birth was a desirable quality on the mother world . . . which was, if one thought about it, somewhat ironical.

"You spliced us into the Bridge System," Angoss said coolly. "You laid down the conditions, take it or leave it. And we took it. Didn't we?"

Almost, Thorkild demanded what the point of that remark was. Then he saw what answer he would get. Abruptly he spun on his heel and departed by the way he had come. Even before the door had closed he heard Angoss say, "Loveling, again—highing the key for my bassest notes have stretched my voice."

Riger's World, Platt's World, Kayowa . . . the layers above were busier, for Platt's and Kayowa were currently inviting settlers rather than just visitors. He saw the activity there with his inward eye as he climbed stairs towards his own floor, topmost in the building, where he ruled. The way he punished his limbs by hurrying up the soft steps which gave back no noise at his tread was intended to be a tribute to his youth, designed to bring him gasping to the highest level. He was young for his fantastically responsible post: when he succeeded Saxena, barely forty. All possible candidates had been evaluated, and he had been . . .

Face it, he told himself. He had been the least unsuitable. But it was always like that nowadays on

Earth. There was never anyone perfectly adapted to any job any more. The jobs had evolved faster than the species that invented them.

At least it was unlikely the strain would undermine him physically. The body he occupied was vastly impressive: nearly two metres tall, hair blond shading to red, eyes piercing blue, build muscular but lean. And this was what people thought of when they thought of Jorgen Thorkild. How could they guess at the weariness which assailed him after barely a year? Psychological strain showed only by hints and clues. Angoss, after their meeting today, would probably be more aware of his true condition than those who worked for him day in, day out, in the same office.

And of those there were a horde.

If you were an Earthside representative for a whole buzzing lively world, you rated a human secretary, as Angoss rated Maida.

If you were the Director, you rated as many as you cared to ask for, and disappointed applicants still had to be turned away.

If you were an Earthside representative, you had a staff of agents here and at home, capable of comprehending your intention from a curt memorandum, authorised to act in your name on the strength of it.

If you were the Director, your staff was numbered in the thousands, and some were lightyears distant.

And you still had to do the work.

A dozen men and women were busy in the anteroom he had to traverse to regain his own sanctum; there was something old-fashioned about their being physically present. But the way the Bridge System was run had been dictated by master psychologists, and so far their judgment had been proven right. Thorkild himself was grateful for this practice; to lay a hand on someone's shoulder now and then . . .

But right now he could not bring himself to acknowledge their greetings with anything more than a smile and nod. Not until he was safely ensconced behind his desk did he speak again, and then it was to the air, activating the circuits with a coded order, and continuing.

"Anything since I've been out?"

"Responsible van Heemskirk called, and will call back in a few minutes," said a sweetly-inflected artificial voice. It always reminded him of his mother's, but he had never dared mention the fact to anyone, since he suspected it must be policy on the part of the machines which actually ran the Bridge City, struggling to puzzle out the whims and preferences of the unpredictable humans to whom they were notionally subservient. Arguing with computers was a special talent, and one which Thorkild feared he might not possess.

"Also Alida Marquis called and wants you to call her. I have a contact series for her. And Inwards Traffic wants to know whether Preacher Rungley will require Earthside surveillance. The request is flagged *immediate*."

Alida . . .

Every time he thought of her, he thought of Saxena, unavoidably, and right now as ever wished he hadn't. A portrait of him hung on the wall, as of all previous holders of this exalted post. It did not show the face of a worried man. Having been taken on the day of his appointment, it rather suggested dedication, enthusiasm, and excitement. So what the hell went wrong?

His own portrait would doubtless imply the same when it was added to the range following his retirement . . . or death.

So what the *hell* went wrong?

The machine said again, with a feigned anxiety, "The request is flagged *immediate*!"

"Oh, yes . . . Let Rungley go on his way but make sure people bring him the most poisonous snakes to be found in all our zoos. Keep a watch on him and let me know as soon as he's hospitalised, then ensure that the media make a splash about it." And that, though it sounded like his own decision, was in fact one made by an untidy, ill-dressed man drinking beer and singing a dirty song. Never mind. It was still his. Whether he fathered it or adopted it.

He wished very much that he could be a father. And that made him think again about Alida. And, in due time, made him wish he hadn't.

The artificial voice was still speaking. "Noted and implemented, Director. May I apply to Wild Conservation if the zoos can't furnish sufficient snakes?"

Oh, these machines were getting too damned smart for comfort! Affecting a bored tone, he said, "Reserve status but authorised."

"Acknowledged. Target zone?"

"Embarrassed enough to head back to Riger's within thirty days."

"Acknowledged. Thank you. Shall I return Alida's call?"

Thorkild felt a stab of foolish anger. Even as he uttered his reply he knew it would prejudice his chances, perhaps beyond hope. He spoke nonetheless.

"No, let her call me back."

"Very good, Director. And—Oh, Responsible van Heemskirk is calling again. Do you wish communication?"

"Ohhh . . . ! Yes, all right."

Responsible van Heemskirk appeared in the office, as though he were sitting in an armchair facing Thorkild's desk. In fact he was suspended in mid-air;

the solido equipment in the Bridge Centre was the finest in existence, but it could not always arrange to have the right piece of furniture in place at the receiving end, so there was half a metre of vacancy beneath his rump.

But one was used to that.

"Day, Jorgen," he said in a cordial tone.

"Day, Moses." Fat as butter and twice as greasy—if any butter were to be found of his dusky South African coloration. No, that was unfair. He was a career politician, and no worse than others of his stamp. He might even really be as affable as he pretended. Only with politicians, how to tell?

"We have these two aspirant worlds," van Heemskirk went on. "Ipewell and Azrael. You haven't forgotten that their delegates are due at the Bridge Centre this afternoon?"

As though he could! Much though he would have liked to . . .

"Moses, you know that if there's one thing I hate—"

"It's showing around parties of giggling outworlders. I know!" The voice from the solido image was soothing. A ripple indicating a sigh moved under the politician's yellow satin robe. "However, this is very different from the ordinary. These are delegates from worlds not yet spliced into the Bridge System, not your run-of-the-mill ambassadors and diplomats. They must know what the Bridges represent already, since that's how they came here, but they haven't signed contracts—"

"They will! Everybody always has!"

"True, I grant you"—inclining his head. "But among the crucial factors which have ensured our thus-far unbroken record of success I would cite the privilege of being shown over the Bridge Centre by its most important personage. Admittedly these delegates are important on their own worlds, but the further out we explore the more backward the societies prove to be—inevitably. And the parties in question strike me as being somewhat overwhelmed by Earth. Your usual warm welcome, your no-nonsense, equal-terms approach, could go a long way towards setting their minds at rest."

"Are you implying that they're suspicious of our motives?"

"You could say that twice and I wouldn't accuse you of exaggeration," van Heemskirk replied in a judicious tone. His manner was disarming; against his will, Thorkild found a smile on his face.

"Very well. I'll do my best. You'll be here at fifteen hundred, isn't that right?"

"As punctually as possible. And don't let the problem get you down. It could be years before we find another outworld. Let alone two within a month of one another!"

True enough. But as van Heemskirk made to cut the circuit, Thorkild checked him, reaching out as though he could take a grip on the intangible image.

"Moses, just a moment!"

"Yes?"

"How many times have you travelled by Bridge?"

"Goodness, I've no idea. But no more often than I could help, except on duty or for occasional vacations. Why?"

"I just wondered."

The politician raised one eyebrow. "I suppose you use the Bridges every day?"

"No." Thorkild couldn't help sounding puzzled. "Like you, when I absolutely have to. And sometimes I wonder why. Until fifteen!"

He watched the image dissolve, then went on staring at the place where it had been.

Half a million people a day, he thought. And I

would rather walk. Who am I? What am I? What are
we?

Saxena's portrait drew his gaze again, and as he
looked at it he found he was thinking about Alida.

II

When the local sun shone on this, the greatest city of the planet Azrael, its harsh radiance seemed incongruous. This morning's early mists, the occasional lift of wind and sift of drizzling rain, were more appropriate.

Jacob Chen drew close the native cloak which concealed his Earthside clothing, tightened the hood about his head to hide his foreign features, and walked circumspect along a narrow alley. The buildings were mostly of dark stone, glinting where the sheen of wet upon their walls caught and somehow reluctantly gave back the glimmer of the occasional street-lights.

There were lights in a few windows, too. Not many. It still lacked half an hour of dawn.

One should not have to think of people as being formed by their climate, not in this age when climate could be controlled. It had been done on more than thirty planets. Here, had the inhabitants neglected to do so because they could not afford to, or because they were ignorant of the means? Hardly. Long before their ancestors departed Earth, the techniques were commonplace and tolerably cheap. No, the decision must have been made as a matter of principle.

But what principle? He did not know; he was baffled by a wall of incomprehension between himself and them. And he was monstrously ashamed. He felt he had failed in his duty by not understanding. Worse still, he had failed by the standards he had set himself, and doubt of his own capability was the fearfullest horror he could imagine.

In the beginning he had fancied that he would find the key in his own ancestors' traditional fatalism; he had rashly assumed that he if anyone could analyse this culture. A local year had ebbed away, and it was autumn again in this hemisphere, as it had been when he arrived aboard the scoutship *Hunting Dog*. Since they preferred to keep the natural seasons, why did these people have no ceremonies to mark the cycle of them? Why was there no public celebration of the spring, or harvest-tide? Why was there no defiance of mid-winter, with lighting of symbolic fires? Such actions were known to stabilise the human psyche, to locate the individual amid the random fluctuation of an adopted world . . .

Yet they did have rituals and ceremonies, and were perfectly prepared to let them be witnessed, and to explain with infinite patience their supposed significance. Only to Jacob Chen, and all those who had come with him from the mother world, they made no sense!

Of late this fact had been costing Chen his sleep, climaxing in this night which he had spent walking at random through the city, seeking with all his senses for some hidden clue.

And found nothing.

He sniffed the air. Bitter smoke. Someone lighting a stove. Grey against grey was spiralling up from the chimney of a house across the way. A window opened. Fearful of being observed, he hurried on-ward, and emerged from the alley into a junction of streets he had not passed before, forming a circus with a blank obelisk in the centre. Seeing it automatically crowded his mind with anthropological data: fertility symbols, upstanding to the sky.

No, it wasn't one. It was merely itself, merely an object. It had not been shaped or polished or submitted to a mason's skills. It had been found exactly in its present form, and erected for no better reason than that it had happened.

Beyond it, one whole side of the circus was occupied by a large drab building, featureless but for a flight of steps and an entrance. He approached it, listening for what he knew would be audible. Sure enough, he detected chanting. Sometimes there was a hiss-and-slap and a groan or cry. Why should the location of a building so important to this culture be signalled by a creation of pure chance? Was he never going to understand these people?

He ascended the five shallow stone steps towards the door. It was huge, six metres high at least, and because it was so difficult to open without power hinges, which he could see it did not have, another smaller door was set in it. This latter stood ajar. After brief hesitation, he stepped inside.

One dim lantern swung in the wind beyond the door, from a low false ceiling which—together with plain native-wood partitions—formed an anteroom with another, sliding, door on the far side. No decoration, no symbolism, no cult-objects . . . As starkly functional as a spaceship's emergency airlock.

And that was correct. What went on here and in other similar places was functional. This was the dynamo that powered the entire society. But the nature of the function eluded him, so that he felt like a savage confronting a computer.

Not to understand—worse yet, to understand wrong!—was what could certainly destroy him.

Giddy with fatigue, moving more by reflex than intention, he slid aside the panel in the interior partition and went into the great hall which occupied most of the high-roofed building.

Here there was no furnishing except plain wooden benches, and again no decoration. There were half a dozen lanterns. The windows, still full of darkness, were tall slits with many small pieces of clear glass set in metal frames. The floor was of rough stone flags. About fifty or sixty people were present, some sitting on the benches with their eyes closed, rocking back and forth and chanting the dull tuneless song he had heard from outside, while a few more lay on the floor unconscious. The benches were disposed to form three sides of a square; in the area between them, at the geometric centre of the hall, four men and two women wearing only coarse kilts were scourging each other with the things that made the hiss-and-slap noise: broad-lashed whips with short thick handles.

That was all.

No one turned to look at him. The only acknowledgment those on the benches accorded the intruder was to draw closer around themselves cloaks similar to the one he was wearing, hiding the whip-marks which—he knew—all of them must bear by now. The ceremony would have begun at sunset, and would continue until daylight brightened the windows.

How could a society be built on this?

Chen looked about him, and shuddered, and returned to the cold unwelcoming street.

But the stream of his thoughts cast up a phrase like a decaying corpse oozing from its mouth the water of a putrid river, stinking of decayed hopes.

I must be wrong ...

He could not bear the possibility. The concept of being wrong was one which he had systematically eliminated from the pattern of his existence. He was a pantologist. A pantologist could not be wrong. A pantologist had insufficient data.

And here if anywhere must be sought the extra data that he needed.

He stopped in his tracks, turned, a great pounding in his chest as though his heart had suddenly grown to twice its normal size and the hardness of iron, clanging at every beat. His belly stretched tight with apprehension, like the skin of a drum.

But he went back up the five steps towards the little door set in the big door, shedding all his clothing bar his cloak.

They came out from the city a few hours after dawn, four men in sweeping black robes, shiny, as if oiled, with fringed fur hats on their heads. They rode like mutes on the way to a funeral in a high-sided car powered by a humming electric motor. When they crossed the boundary of the spaceport they slowed the vehicle so that a group of forewarned members of the port staff could fall in behind, walking stately through the morning rain.

Captain Lucy Inkoos descended the scoutship's ramp to greet them. They had notified her of Chen's fate with regret that seemed genuine. And it wasn't for her to judge.

Along with four of her officers she stood hatless in the downpour. Drops spotted and then flowed together on the red fabric of her uniform. Some of her ancestors had cast the Benin bronzes; her face, fine-boned, high-cheeked, was as impassive as a bronze idol while she waited for the approach of the cortège.

The high-sided car halted. Stiffly, like awkward but silent machines, the four black-robed men emerged from it. One walked forward to face the captain. He was at least her equal in height, and his high-crowned hat added thirty centimetres to that, so as to give the effect of immense stature. He was not looking down at her, yet she seemed to hear his voice from far overhead.

He said, "We have brought the corpse of your colleague."

Captain Inkoos nodded. "Arrangements have been made for its reception."

Around her the four officers shifted from foot to foot.

"We regret this," the man said. "As I have had the story, he volunteered to join one of our rituals. In the hall near the circus of the obelisk. By chance a participant decided to take action the very moment he joined the group. And . . . he is as you see."

His companions, with help from some of the port staff, had opened the back of the car and were now lifting out the remains of Jacob Chen. His body was wrapped in a shroud of black cloth, but when the light fell full it showed a reddish stain over what must be the position of his heart.

"The man who killed him"—Captain Inkoos heard the voice seem now to come not merely from a great distance in space, but also far away in time—"will of course be dealt with. Would you wish to send representatives to witness the execution? It will take place tomorrow."

Captain Inkoos repressed a shudder. She said, "No!" And, realising how brusque and discourteous her tone must have sounded, went on hastily, "We accept that Chen had no business intervening in your ritual. He left the ship by himself, telling no one where he was going. He brought his fate on himself."

"His wishing to join the ritual," the man said. "We have no objection, you understand. It is open to all. Only we do not think he knew the reason for joining. And he did not find out."

Captain Inkoos felt her broad flat lips press together, narrowing, as she studied the face of the man before her. The fringe of his hat concealed most of his forehead, but the rain had gathered the fur together into stringy bunches, and she could guess at the location of his hairline. He had a high intellectual's forehead, a sensitive mouth, the hollow cheeks of an ascetic—

And he was inviting her to a public execution!

It was not her business to understand, for which she was profoundly grateful. She could only curse Jacob Chen for wasting himself, and utter polite thanks to the other men in black shiny robes when the corpse had been delivered to the ramp, and remember to ask for a transcript of the trial for inclusion in her report to headquarters.

"There will be no trial," the man said. "I myself have conducted the prescribed investigation. I am a custodian of propriety. I think you would perhaps say magistrate. It was in the course of ritual, in plain view of all. When one does that, he is deliberate. It is to restore reality to existence by terminating it. There is nothing else."

That wall they had battered for a year, since first contact. Captain Inkoos wondered whether Jacob Chen had breached it in his last moments, before his life flooded from the knife-hole in his chest. The four officers moved to lift the body on to a nulgrav stretcher; one placed his hand incautiously, and when he took it away his fingertips were marked with rusty blood.

These are people, she said to herself. They had ancestors in common with me. All human beings are at least cousins. All human beings can talk to one another and make sense. This world when it was rediscovered was assumed to be much like any other—and why not? There was this spaceport, with a fleet of ferry-ships which travelled to the local asteroids, mining and refining, and to a scientific observatory on the major satellite, and the living-standard was tolerable if a trifle drab compared with most other colonised worlds'. And considering the long gap since previous contact with other branches of the race, the language spoken here was remarkably close to Standard Earthside.

Except that it wasn't. The words appeared to make sense, and then somehow, as if they had been twisted through another dimension . . .

Which was why she had had to send for Jacob Chen, because she needed a master pantologist to transcend this barrier of non-comprehension. Only—!

She glanced up the ramp. The body was being guided out of sight by the four officers—awkwardly, for it was no part of their normal duties to handle the inertia-free slab of a nulgrav stretcher, and out of habit they kept treating it as though it, and its burden, *must* weigh something.

There would be an inquiry. What would be its verdict? You didn't order a pantologist to account for his movements. You appealed to him, describing a problem in the hope that it might strike him as sufficiently absorbing to warrant the application of his talents. In a word: a pantologist knew what to do better than anybody else.

But could be just as dead as anybody else.

And if Chen had failed, who was going to solve the problem?

The black-robed men and the port staff stood silent; only the sound of the rain could be heard, and the tread of feet on the metal ramp as the officers returned to their former stations.

No one would put blame on her, Captain Inkoos thought. But would they blame Chen himself, a man who could out-reason the most advanced computers, who could spot the flaws in logic committed by humanity's most logical machines? What about these men in black robes and fur hats? Could it be called their fault? Could anyone be blamed for his or her born nature?

Yet tired old Earth would insist on being told at least the reason for this death. At a time when half its citizens doubted the purpose of continuing existence, when the Bridge System was the only thing that brought any sort of novelty into their lives—and the relish of novelty was wearing stale—there could easily be a wave of desperation, and it would as usual be graphed in terms of suicides.

That would come if no reason could be offered. Ancient Earth credited one law above all others: cause and effect. The effect could be endured, provided that one understood the cause.

How could that law not apply on Azrael?

At an unspoken command, the port staff dispersed towards the administrative buildings, low-crouched at the edge of the landing-ground. The man she had been talking to said, "We regret it, you understand."

"I believe you."

"We regret existence," the man said. He glanced at his companions, and all four of them climbed back into their car.

Captain Inkoos watched them go with such dignity, and thought of them as they might perhaps be today, or tomorrow—stripped to the waist, offering themselves to pain. Pain is the sole reality, they said. Pleasure can be negated; even boredom, the neutral, featureless state, makes pleasure unthinkable. But the happiest can be hurled to the depths of misery by the stab of a rotting tooth, or the lash of a whip on the back. Unite reality to consciousness, they said, by using pain. And if that ultimately fails, one may invoke the last reality of all by taking such action as to cause his death. Here, as on many worlds more backward than Earth, they killed people for murder. Slay in the sight of witnesses, and in your turn be slain. (And the one you pick on may by chance be Jacob Chen, unique, genius, pantologist . . .)

So much was clear. What remained a mystery was this: how could a society continue to exist, when its most fundamental creed was anti-life?

She grew aware that her senior aide, Commander Kwan, had moved closer so he could speak without being overheard as the members of the brief cortège dispersed.

He murmured, "What are we to make of them?"

Captain Inkoos shrugged, not willing to attempt an answer.

"Will we ever be able to get on with them?" Kwan persisted.

"Ask the future," Captain Inkoos sighed, and marched up the ramp, her hard boots making a sharp tap-tap like the drum-beat for a funeral parade.

III

Like most worlds with characteristics fitting them for human occupation, Ipewell had one large satellite and a G-type primary. But Ipewell had no moon, and no sun.

They were Mother's Night Eye and Mother's Day Eye.

Formerly he had had no chance of being allowed out on his own unless one of Mother's Eyes was open. But by behaving so well lately that his family had almost grown suspicious, Lork (Garria-third-boy) had contrived to stretch and stretch the periods when he could be out of sight without people asking where he had got to.

This evening: the big risk, the staking of all.

There was a gap of four whole hours today between the disappearance of the Day Eye into the red clouds of sunset and the opening of the Night Eye among the stars. Consumed half by terror and half by astonishment at his own bravery, he slipped out of the great yard of the family homestead via the alley between the dairy and the granary, and darted for a forbidden path among the riverside bushes. It was forbidden because it had once been a creekcat run, but no one had seen a creekcat here in living memory.

Cautiously at first, then with increasing speed as he drew further away from home and the risk of being heard, he made his way around two bends of the river. Finally he paused where a blaze had been cut in the thick spongy stem of a brellabush.

"Jeckin?" he whispered. "You there?"

Jeckin (Fabia-eighth-boy) rose from shadow, sighing with relief. "I thought for certain you'd been turned back," he said. "I don't know how long I've been waiting, but it felt like half eternity. I expected the Night Eye to open any moment!"

"Custom forbid!" Lork exclaimed. He spat on the ground and stamped three times—not because he really believed in such superstitions, but because when so much was at stake it made sense to take all possible precautions. "But we'll have to hurry anyway. Let's go."

Jeckin nodded and parted the bushes carefully. They crept between the heavy drooping leaves and emerged into meadows planted with Earthside grass, which rolled unbroken to the skyline. A long way ahead there could be seen a reddish glow. That marked their destination.

They began to run.

Ten minutes later they were too close to the glow to go on running unnoticed. Jeckin pointed at a clump of maxage and Lork grunted agreement. Together they dived for its shelter, panting to recover their breath. Then they eased forward on knees and elbows up a shallow rise, and . . .

"Told you we could see the starship from here!" Jeckin crowed softly.

"It's big!" Lork whispered. "How many people aboard?"

"I've heard it's a thousand, but I don't believe it. You *couldn't*."

Lork wasn't so sure; to him, this vessel looked large enough to swallow cities. But he was in no mood to argue. All he wanted to do was feast his eyes.

Dull-gleaming in the last of the twilight, the ship rested atop a hundred-metre mound. It was perfectly spherical except for a vertical spike pointing towards the geosynchronous communication-relay satellite it had left in orbit as it came down, which now shone in the night sky of Ipewell in a manner Lork and Jeckin found incomprehensible and most other people found blasphemous. How dare these newcomers deface Mother's domain?

Ipewell was the only human-occupied world so far discovered which had totally lost all knowledge of space-travel, even the most rudimentary kind. Even folk-tales concerning Earth had been rigidly suppressed.

But it was because these strangers knew how to defy Mother, to the extent of planting a new star in the welkin, that the boys had plucked up the courage to come and visit them. If they were caught, they would most certainly be castrated. And the operation would be carried out with red-hot tongs. It was therefore not a journey to be undertaken lightly.

Trying not even to breathe too loud, Lork went on staring. Now his vision had adjusted, he could see that the reddish glow came from portable lights at the foot of the mound, where had been set up a temporary village of prefabricated huts.

"Think we ought to go down and find someone?" he suggested at last. To run this risk and simply lie in hiding . . .

"Someone's coming!" Jeckin answered. "Don't you see?"

Straining his eyes—he had always been rather short-sighted and spectacles were reserved for girls— Lork finally made out two figures moving shadowy on the grassland. For a horrifying moment he thought they were heading purposefully this way; then they turned aside, and he realised they were simply out for a stroll. Nonetheless, the trend of their path was in this direction, and shortly he heard a woman's voice tinged with amusement saying something and completing it with laughter.

Oh, no. It *would* have to be women they met first on this dangerous expedition! Imagine a woman hearing them with sympathy, even the *different* kind of woman rumour reported as being aboard the starship!

Almost, he bolted for home, but Jeckin caught him firmly by the leg, and instants later he found his assumption wrong: not two women, but a woman and a man. The latter's gruffer voice carried less well than his companion's.

"What shall we do?" Lork whispered.

"Stand up and show ourselves, of course, as soon as they come close! Isn't that the whole idea?"

Well, maybe. Except that the couple already seemed to have come as close as they intended. They were in a shallow dip overlooked from where Lork and Jeckin lay. Glancing around, deciding the spot was sufficiently secluded, the man unrolled something mattress-like which he had been carrying. The woman helped him straighten it on the ground. Lork's scalp began to prickle. Surely they weren't about to—

But at this range he could clearly see that the woman wasn't pregnant. Indeed, by Ipewell standards she was skinny. The man, on the other hand, was a fine specimen such as any mother would have trouble keeping to herself. It was an odd pairing, in his view; still, perhaps the starfolk had compulsory arrangements about fatherhood. Lork understood vaguely that the way of life the visitors followed differed from what he was accustomed to, but he had no experience to help him imagine how.

The man turned to the woman and put out his arms. They embraced.

"Oh, no!" Lork exploded, and leapt to his feet.

The man and woman sprang apart, snatching at their waists. Two powerful lights—seeming to the terrified Lork at least as brilliant as the Day Eye—transfixed him and Jeckin. Miserably the latter too stood up, muttering curses.

After a pause, the man spoke in Ipewell dialect. He said, "So! A couple of peeping janes!"

"No . . . uh . . . *no!*" Lork babbled, and realised for the first time that there wasn't a respectful form of address for male superiors in Ipewell usage. Men, being unable to reproduce, were by definition inferior. Yet it seemed wrong to speak to a man from the stars as an equal. "We just wanted to—uh . . ."

How to hammer into words the impulse that had driven them to defy the personal order of Mother Uskia, forbidding all males to approach the starship?

He was saved the trouble. The woman spoke up, and reflex made him answer instantly.

"Who are you, anyway?"

Shaking, he gave their names.

"Jeckin (Fabia-eighth-boy)?" the woman repeated. "I've heard about your family. Life must be pretty fair hell for you and your brothers, isn't it?"

Well, that wasn't the sort of remark you'd ordinarily expect from a woman! Encouraged, Jeckin burst out, "Yes—yes! For my mother-in-fact has eleven children, which should bring her great honour, but we are all male, all of us, and she is past bearing now and the shame of having no daughters stains the family!"

Jeckin squeezed his friend's arm reassuringly. He knew very well how unbearable Fabia made life for her children because of their sex. But what sort of woman could share the same point of view?

The two boys stood silent for a while, listening but not understanding as the couple from the ship exchanged some half-audible remarks. What snatches reached their ears made little sense: something about restoration of the genetic balance, male infanticide and relative hormone probability.

At last the man turned with a smile and spoke in a friendly voice.

"Well, now you're here, you'd best explain what you came for. Sit down—no, over here on the mattress; it's plenty big enough. Let's hear your story."

Timidly, they complied.

Fay Logan paid attention as best she could. This was not quite how she had meant to spend this evening . . . She and her companion had extinguished their lanterns, and now it was barely possible to make out the boys' features, but she could tell they were good-looking—dark-haired, probably rather dark-skinned like most of Ipewell's people, and about the same age, fifteen or sixteen. And intelligent. And frustrated.

Then her mind wandered and she found she was staring at Hans Demetrios. He sat cross-legged, head cocked to one side, absolutely taut with concentration. A pang went through her.

This was where his interest lay. Not in her. Not in any human being, not even himself—only in the pattern of problems which the human race was creating as it fumbled its way across the universe.

Half-jokingly they said there was a new humanity evolving and Hans Demetrios belonged to it, and Jacob Chen, and a handful of others: as though a racial subconscious were reacting over generations to ensure that people would continue to outstrip the prowess of their machines. If so, theirs must be a hungry breed. One could see it. Hans Demetrios was physically not in the least like Jacob Chen, and yet the thing they had in common showed in their starving-bright eyes, their tense cheek-muscles, their ability to attain utter repose when their minds were engaged in the sort of analysis no one else would dare to tackle.

Pantologists, they were called. The name meant, approximately, students of everything. Hans was young but already outstanding in their company. He would go far. Already he was out of reach of Fay Logan, who had thought she loved him.

She had tried to keep in touch. She knew the tools with which people investigated the cosmos; she understood the superimbecility of computers, which generations of cunning disguise had transformed into what ordinary folk mistook for superior intelligence. She worked with them all the time. With terrible exhausting concentration and provided she was not disturbed by so much as the drift of a dust-mote across her vision, she could voice-program a computer to the extent of a few thousand words before there came the inevitable mild inquiry concerning an implicit contradiction, to be verified and remedied. Whereas, so rumour held, Jacob Chen could speak a program of a million words or more without an error, taking a month over it, and never ask for prompting or even make a note. All in the head. All at once.

As for Hans . . . Today she had seen him finish the program for the Ipewell Bridge, not because it had been contracted for but purely to keep himself occupied. He had spent a fortnight on it, ten hours a day, pausing for meals and sleep, and made not a single error. Not even one, that might have helped to prove he was still human.

One could walk into the room where he was at

work, and he would look up when he had adjusted to the need to be distracted, and nod and smile, and keep right on going.

He lives in a different universe, Fay thought. And it's so unfair that he can still come back and talk to us, and I can't reach out to where he's gone . . .

"I'll explain," Hans was saying confidentially to the two boys. "I suppose you've wondered how people so much like yourselves can come down from the sky—yes? Well, to put it as simply as possible, it's because those lights you see in the night sky are actually suns, like the one which warms this planet by day. You know about planets, yes? Good! I wasn't sure how much boys get told around here!" And a warm chuckle which made them visibly relax.

Unfair! Unfair!

"We started to spread out from our first planet, the Earth, many centuries ago. I won't try and give you all the reasons—sometimes they were political, sometimes economic, but mainly they were just a case of good old-fashioned restlessness. After all, our ancestors had been stuck on one ball of mud for millions of years, and it sort of felt like time for a change. And Ipewell is one of the places people came to, determined to colonise and change it. But a planet is big, and human beings are small. You need a lot of people to conquer a new world, many more than can be kept alive in a single starship. So usually the colonists took with them sperm and ova banks and artificial wombs, so as to be able to breed very rapidly as soon as they found a habitable world.

"As we've pieced it together, some terrible disaster—perhaps an earthquake, or a tidal wave—destroyed all this kind of equipment shortly after the first landing here on Ipewell. Which was a real tragedy, because this is one of the most ideal planets we've ever come across: no major natural predators, no serious local diseases, nothing that couldn't be handled with ordinary enterprise and common sense. In fact, this is *the* most Earthlike planet out of the forty we so far know about."

Impressed, the boys gave simultaneous nods.

"But to colonise it, your ancestors desperately needed a large-scale population. Given that they couldn't breed from the artificial wombs, they converted female fertility into a fetish, and fertile women assumed the dominant position in your society. Of course, the inherited effect of millions of years of evolution as a bisexual species couldn't be undone overnight, but they tried their uttermost to make it so, even to the extent of inventing legends about the Greatest Mother, with her Night Eye and her Day Eye. That's all they are, you know: just stories, which someone thought up to justify the matriarchy—uh, excuse me—rule by women."

The boys winced in unison. Since both the Eyes were of course closed at the moment, though, the blasphemy naturally went unpunished . . . which was heartening.

"Eventually," Hans pursued, "even the fastest ships we could construct—even though they broke what for generations we had regarded as a universal law concerning the speed of light, but I won't bother you with that—even our fastest ships proved inadequate to keep up our contact with all the planets that our race had spread to, and for quite a long time we were completely out of touch except with the very closest. And we could only afford to make one or two flights a year to and from those.

"About a hundred years ago, that all changed, with the invention of the Bridge System. Either of you know Mother Uskia?"

Licking their lips, Lork and Jeckin exchanged glances. To them, that was rather like being asked whether they knew the Lord God Almighty. But Lork eventually said, "Well, I guess we must have seen her. And we sure have heard about her!"

"So you must be aware that she isn't on Ipewell right now?"

The word had been put around: that the Greatest Mother was keeping her Eye on things until Uskia's return. Lork boldly nodded.

"They told us she had gone to heaven, because she was so perfect after having seven female children!"

"Well—ah—not exactly." Hans repressed a smile. "At the moment she's on the planet our starship comes from, Earth. She's there to negotiate the splicing-in of Ipewell to the Bridge System. By means of it, matter—including living people—can be transported from world to world . . . though of course the most important thing we transfer is always knowledge.

"We Earthsiders have made it our great task to re-unite scattered humanity on all the planets to which it has now wandered. This is not something other worlds must pay for. It's our service to the human race. It's our greatest ambition. Anyone can go by Bridge to anywhere he or she chooses, provided he or she carries no arms and no sickness—and we can cure almost every kind of sickness now. That's the sole condition we lay down: that *anyone* can use the Bridges."

"But suppose—" Lork found himself fumbling. "Suppose someone had done something wrong, and wanted to use the Bridge to get away?"

"To escape punishment, you mean? Ah! That's a very acute question! But give me an example."

"Well—uh—I mean if they caught us here, talking to you, they'd condemn us to be . . ." Words failed him.

"Punished for what crime? Talking to a new friend? Under the laws of Earth that's not a crime! Of course, if you'd killed somebody—"

"Killed somebody?" Jeckin burst out. "You mean like killing a steer for beef? But people don't! Why should they? You can't eat people!" He stumbled terribly over the concept; it was so unspeakably foreign to his way of thinking.

"I think that's why Ipewell is going to join the Bridge System. Which operates under the laws of Earth. So far, none of your laws has seemed to contradict ours, except the ones that apply to disadvantaged males. And that sort of thing, of course, we simply won't tolerate."

"If you built a Bridge here," Lork ventured, "could . . . could we use it?"

"If by the laws of Earth you're of the age of discretion, the answer's yes."

Fay heard the two boys sigh as one. Her own sigh was not noticed, except by herself.

When at last the boys headed for home, hurrying because it was time for the Night Eye to open, they went in stunned silence. They felt like slaves whose shackles had suddenly been struck off.

"Do you believe it?" Jeckin said when they reached the path beside the river where they had to separate.

"I want to," Lork answered soberly.

"So do I."

For a while they listened to the plash of the water, staring at one another as though to search out their sincerity.

At last Jeckin said awkwardly, "Lork, if it does happen, if they make this—this Bridge he talked about, and we can go to other worlds from here . . . Well, shall we?"

"Mother Uskia and all her sisters couldn't stop me!" was Lork's reply.

Jeckin glanced up between the dense leaves of the

brellabush. The Night Eye was rising in the sky. He said, "She's watching!"

"Let her," Lork answered. "I think she's going to have to watch a lot of things more abominable than what you and I are doing."

Jeckin chuckled throatily. He clapped his friend on the arm and slid into the dark. Lork turned away likewise. On the way home he began to sing.

IV

From a godlike vantage-point, seventy metres above the floor of the Bridge Centre transit-hall, Jorgen Thorkild looked down on people milling beneath his feet and thought of insects. Or signals in the circuits of a computer. Or chemicals being processed in a factory. Anything except human beings. At this range they had no personal identity. Anonymous as molecules and almost as numerous, they were piped and channelled and directed by the impersonal decision of machines.

If this were Olympus and I were Zeus with thunderbolts to hurl, I wouldn't kill people. I'd just alter a few entries in the memory-banks.

What the hell ever happened to human importance?

Behind him the door leading on to the vantage platform hushed open. He turned, composing his face into a polite mask.

First in view was Moses van Heemskirk, who never missed an opportunity like this. He couldn't have been prouder of the Bridge System if he'd invented the principle himself. By this time, perhaps he thought he had.

About sixty people followed him, in two distinct

groups of roughly equal size—but that from Ipewell consisted wholly of women, whereas that from Azrael was exclusively composed of men. Both were obviously stratified within themselves: the leaders had brought their respective retinues, because they still relied on human sides and secretaries. On the rare occasions when he had had to make a formal visit to another planet, Thorkild had worn his "retinue" in a simple belt full of microcircuitry. Here within the Bridge Centre he did not even have to do that.

It crossed his mind that the answer to his mental question of a moment ago might perhaps be sought in the fact that nowadays the Earthside élite found it more convenient (more congenial?) to keep company with predictable machines. He himself was resentful of the need to turn out for these—these tourists. Any of a hundred people on his staff could have handled this chore with genuine enthusiasm . . .

Well, having delegates from two aspirant worlds at once was unprecedented, and it was happening during his term of office. He must make the most of that.

The vantage platform, and the impervious bubble enclosing it, had a refractive index equal to that of air. Most of the visitors hung back even when van Heemskirk marched forward, hand outstretched towards Thorkild. Two did not, and they were plainly the most important.

"Day, Jorgen!" van Heemskirk boomed. "Let me present to you the honoured delegates of the latest worlds to aspire to membership of our interstellar community—Mother Uskia of Ipewell, and Lancaster Long of the planet Azrael! Friends, this is Director Jorgen Thorkild, whose untiring work in the service of the Bridge System puts everyone on forty planets in his debt!"

Usually Thorkild turned van Heemskirk's fulsome

flattery with some amusing and self-depreciatory remark. Today he couldn't think of one. He merely
shrugged and bowed, earning a frown from the fat
man. He knew what that was due to: the same reason
that had made van Heemskirk present the delegates to
him, not the other way around, although their relative
status on their home worlds was probably far superior
to Thorkild's on Earth. In van Heemskirk's eyes,
Earthside prestige counted above all else. He never
tired of reminding people that Earth got there first.

Got where? To what purpose?

Cautious, the rank and file were spreading across
the vantage platform, whispering in awe at the sheer
scale of the transit-hall. So might they well; it was the
largest building on any human planet. But Thorkild
had heard such ooh-ing and ahh-ing before. He
concentrated his attention on the two he had just been
introduced to.

Mother Uskia: a flat-faced, dark woman in a tight
white shirt and tighter white trousers cut to show off
a bulging melon-belly. Pregnant, and proud of it. On
Ipewell fertility was emblematic of social status—
hence the honorific Mother before her name. Clipped
to her collar was a microphone, and a thin flex led
from it down the open neck of her shirt, vanishing
between fat mounds of breast. Presumably she was
making a sonic record of her trip to Earth, though
why she should prefer a sound-only to the equally
available and more informative solido version was a
mystery.

And Lancaster Long: immensely tall, a hand's
breadth more than Thorkild himself, wearing a splendid purple robe and a cylindrical hat of white fur. His
complexion was rather sallow. His high-arched nose
and sharp dark eyes lent him the appearance of a bird
of prey.

Being awestruck could be left to underlings. Both

these leaders moved to the furthest edge of the platform and gazed down, evaluating what they saw. After a pause, Long said, "How much bigger is this place than the station on Mars that we were brought to first?"

"In terms of handling capacity? Sixty or eighty thousand times," Thorkild answered.

There was a silence. Shortly van Heemskirk began to fidget. He did not easily endure inactivity. "Uh . . . Jorgen!" he suggested. "Tell our friends about the System. Whatever you think would interest them. After all, it's most impressive, isn't it?"

What would they not already know? What could van Heemskirk imagine they did not know? They had been under instruction before they left home, then on Mars, then again since being forwarded to Earth . . . But Thorkild obeyed, and began to recite worn facts, parrot-style.

"The station on Mars doesn't have to be any larger. It's dedicated solely to the needs of people like yourself who have to undergo quarantine and prepare themselves psychologically for a first visit to Earth. Apart from the times when we are newly in contact with an aspirant world, it's on standby—idling, as you might say—except when someone reports a risk of epidemic disease. That's the one thing we are constantly on guard against: the chance that some microorganism on a world we have not yet fully explored might prove to be fatal to human beings on an interstellar scale. Then volunteers present themselves and from our computer resources we construct the necessary counter-agent. We haven't failed to do so yet, and it's as well, because once your worlds are spliced into the Bridge System you'll have unlimited access to it. Some idea of its scale can be gained by looking around this hall. Here we have Bridges direct to all the inhabited worlds, plus well over a hundred more which link us to the starships constantly hunting for others that we haven't yet re-contacted. We build on a generous scale. We expect our present equipment to remain adequate for at least another hundred years."

His words ground to a halt. He was acutely aware of Mother Uskia's microphone, and of her intense, suspicious manner. What could someone like that find interesting in these dry, dead-leaf words? On a planet like hers, human beings were not yet reduced to the state where they could be processed like a flow of information, faceless, averaged, present or absent merely as statistical variations. About the only thing he could say to these people which they would not already have heard was something which van Heemskirk and those above him would regard as disastrously inappropriate. He could talk about the way that humans, in the view of the machinery which actually ran the Bridge System, were so predictable that daily traffic-flow could be forecast with an accuracy of plus or minus point oh-one per cent.

What would Mother Uskia's reaction be if he were to come straight out with it and say that his job, in the ultimate analysis, was to ensure that their planets also conformed to the rigid pattern?

And how about Long? He wore an expression which defied scrutiny. Perhaps it reflected boredom. Probably it did. The notion behind bringing these delegations to the actual Bridge Centre was to drive home the physical size of the operation, but surely anyone with a normal imagination could work that out in advance, and the mere sight of this place and the people swarming through it could never be half as impressive as what had already been done to the visitors. It had been proved to them that they could cross a hundred lightyears at a single step. After that, there was nothing . . . was there?

Now he was looking at Long, he found it impos-

sible to tear his gaze away. Why? For his height?
There were many Earthsiders who could overtop him
by half a metre. For his leanness and his eagle nose?
But anybody now might be as fat or thin as he or she
chose, and wear any face that appealed to the individual's fancy. For the subconscious associations of his
garb, stretching back into classical antiquity? True,
purple was the traditional princes' colour, but one
might buy garments that shifted through a thousand
colours in a day and began again on the morrow
without repeating.

No, the reason was something inward. A question
of personality. Long had—what to call it?—an air of
presence. Yes, that was it. As though he were *more
here* than Thorkild or van Heemskirk or Mother
Uskia, certainly *more here* than any of the flowing
molecule-people on the transit floor so far below.

Unexpectedly Long turned his head and met
Thorkild's eyes directly. In the dark abysm of his
irises, the Earthman thought, it would be possible to
lose oneself as though in space.

Beginning to be seriously alarmed, van Heemskirk
spoke up again. "Jorgen, suppose you tell us about the
people we can see down there—who they are, where
they're bound for. After all, it's one thing to be
shown the bald statistics, and quite another to be here
and actually watch it happening!"

Yes, of course he might do that. It hadn't occurred
to him. It hadn't occurred to him to look away after
meeting Long's gaze, either. When he did so, he felt
an unreal click—no, not a click, that was wrong, but
something . . . He hunted memory, and located the
image he was after: the sense of reluctant yielding,
amounting almost to a soundless snap, when you draw
apart a pair of magnets.

Knowing the transit schedules by heart for at least a

week in advance, surely he ought to be able to pick out one or two groups down there and say something about them . . . Ah, there was a straggling line of a hundred-odd men and women brilliant in uniform scarlet. He knew who they must be.

Activating the distorter on the enclosing bubble so that the area in question was abruptly magnified, he said, "Well, for example, there goes the crew of the scoutship *Eridanus*—the relief crew, that is, returning to duty after furlough. Very probably you already know about the system we operate, having two crews for every scoutship, rotating at intervals because it's a lonely and sometimes rather boring job to search the stars for planets like your own, cut off from the rest of the human community. Well, like yours were until recently . . ."

But they must have been told this over and over! Why waste his breath?

Badly worried now by Thorkild's peculiar incoherence, van Heemskirk hastened to cover for him. "It's the most remarkable achievement of our species!" he declaimed, using his public orator's voice. "From here, invisible links reach out across the lightyears to unite planet with planet as the strong bonds of affection unite a family. Yes, precisely, for in spite of temporary separation we are one great family after all, are we not?"

Prompt on his beginning to speak, Mother Uskia had turned, making sure her microphone was aligned to catch his words. With more discernment, Long disregarded the politician's fit of orotundity. As soon as it was over, he addressed Thorkild.

"It would appear to be a complex and demanding post that you hold, Director!"

"It is!" van Heemskirk assured him. "One of the most responsible in the galaxy!"

Long did not even shift his gaze to acknowledge

the interruption; van Heemskirk registered the snub, and flushed. A stir of amusement coloured Thorkild's grey thoughts. If Long could take van Heemskirk aback so easily, he must be a remarkable individual.

Remembering belatedly that the original question had been aimed at himself, he gave a nod.

"And are you satisfied?" Long pursued.

"Satisfied?" Thorkild revolved the word in his mind. "Not yet. I guess I shan't be until all the worlds where human beings have settled are tied into the Bridge System. And possibly not even then."

"As far as one can tell at present," Long observed, "this may already have occurred, or be on the verge of doing so. I gather it has been a decade since the last new planet was, as you say, tied in. But set aside the unknowable, the possibility that the Bridge System may already have expanded to its limit. What I meant to ask you was rather whether your work is satisfying. Does that make my intention clearer?"

It would, if I knew what satisfaction was . . .

This is the nature of my job: pipe people from here to there, shove freight around in massive quantities, stand foster-father to decisions taken by a beery drunkard singing a dirty song—when what I really want is to be a father, albeit of a chance-got child. Even taking my own decisions would be a surrogate! But all of them, every last single mortal one of them, are constrained! They are forced on me! I am denied the liberty of being wrong!

Had Saxena suffered this agony? Was this the reason he had killed himself? It wasn't obviously the agony of being rejected by Alida . . .

But aloud he said, "The work is there and because I can do it, I do do it. So far as that goes, I guess it's satisfying."

"The way I understand the matter," Long said, the corners of his mouth turning down to signal disapproval, "you are in charge of what has gradually become Earth's prime reason for continuing. The Bridge System has repeatedly been described to us as the greatest gift the mother planet has ever offered to her children."

The turn of phrase he employed attracted Uskia's complete attention; perhaps it was deliberate, perhaps casual . . .

"Given that you are in overall control of this operation, it should follow that you enjoy the greatest personal fulfilment experienced by anyone in the whole of history. Yet I sensed, a moment ago, that you did not wholly concur with the way Responsible van Heemskirk defined the Bridges—like, he said, bonds of affection that connect the human family. Well?"

Uskia, as usual, angled her microphone to catch Thorkild's reply. Perhaps it was the sudden irritating mannerism which provoked him into rapping out words before he had thought through what he planned to say.

"It's more like the groping of a barnacle, or the web of a spider," he blurted. "If you really want to know! Or even less purposeful than that, even less rational—maybe like the stems of a climbing plant feeling around for something to latch on to and twine around, without the blindest hint of what it's doing it *for*!"

"Jorgen!" cried van Heemskirk, appalled, and started forward. He was checked by Uskia.

"One moment!" she said. "Director Thorkild"—and it was plain from the way she twisted her mouth that she had not yet accustomed herself to speaking politely to a male—"be so kind as to explain what the things are which you compared the Bridge System to: a barnacle and a spider's web. On Ipewell we have neither, although certain creatures in our local eco-structure are analogous."

"If you know that much," Thorkild retorted, "what else can I add?"

A scowl creased Uskia's flat face. "*I* know!" she snapped. "But my daughter must know too!"

She drew the zipper of her tight-stretched shirt down to her waist, and Thorkild saw that the flex from the microphone, held in place by adhesive tape, led to a button-size speaker plugged into her navel, turned inward to address the growing foetus.

Thorkild tried to prevent himself from grinning, but the muscles strained in his cheeks. Activating the distorter again, he gestured at the magnified images it cast on the bubble wall.

"See the grayish crowd? They're emigrants, bound for Platt's World and Kayowa. Eight thousand a day and—"

No good. The idea of the speaker plugged into her navel! You can't start educating them too young! *Wowph!*

And the hooting hysterical laughter began and seemed it would never stop. He managed to force his eyes open three times in succession: once—van Heemskirk looking fit to burst; twice—Uskia, face contorted with rage at the insult he had offered her; thrice—Lancaster Long, looking like the dark angel after whom his planet had been named.

Then the laughter filled his eyes with tears and blinded him.

V

In theory all of Earth's business could for centuries have been conducted at a distance: solido projections could be supplemented even by pheromone synthesisers, which deluded the nose, as well as the eyes and ears, that the other party to the conversation was physically present.

In practice some deeply-ingrained atavism rendered it, if not strictly necessary, then at any rate desirable, to hold face-to-face discussions. Possibly it was because on the subconscious level, what was to be done acquired a gloss of additional importance if one undertook a journey to discuss it. The sense of purpose during the trip reinforced attention and concentration, even though it might also entrain tiredness.

Alida Marquis had sometimes wondered—though strictly privately, only aloud to her most intimate friends—whether the speed and ease of travel by Bridge was what made it fundamentally unsatisfying. Few people realised, but it was thanks to her that even starship crews returning to duty had to wait on line in the single vast transit-hall which handled the off-world trade for the entire planet. Earth was rich enough to have built dozens of Bridge Centres, but in order to preserve at least a semblance of a "real" journey people were still obliged to make their way by old-fashioned methods to their interstellar departure-point.

Except, of course, if one happened to work in the Bridge Centre. There, forty worlds were within walking distance. How could such a marvel become a commonplace fact of daily existence? Yet it had, and there was something essentially wrong about the situation. It smelt of crisis. She had tried to explain her forebodings to Thorkild, but he had always evaded the subject, rather as though he were afraid it might compel him to continue to a discussion of Saxena's fate. In its turn, that would inevitably lead to the question of his relationship with Alida, and she was still reluctant to talk about it. To have your lover of a decade kill himself without warning, without appealing for help . . .

Well, perhaps her premonitions of disaster were illusory, due to that shock.

But she could not help feeling worried about Thorkild. Of late he had grown so—so remote . . . He no longer even made the routine passes at her which, on his appointment, he had indulged in not so much because he desired her—or so she felt—as because, taking over Saxena's post, he expected the perquisites which went with the job.

It was, admittedly, customary for professional colleagues to enjoy sexual contact, and Alida had done so with all the members of the Bridge City Planning Committee, of which she was chairman *ex officio* in her capacity as Supervisor of Inter-world Relations. She was nearly seventy, but she could have passed for thirty by the standards of the pre-galactic age; tall, stately, deep-voiced, with a laser-keen mind, she would ordinarily have been pleased at Thorkild's attentions. After all, a man appointed to the Directorship at forty must be a very remarkable person.

If only he were not so obsessed by the mystery of Saxena's death, as she herself was . . . if only he had been able to jar her out of it with a convincing explanation . . .

She must stop this, and at once! There was business to transact, and the four other members of the committee had fallen silent, as though expecting to be called to order.

They were in her office in the highest tower overlooking the Bridge City. From the windows it could be seen spread out to the skyline and beyond: the place where forty worlds met face-to-face as this committee was doing. It was the ambition of everyone on Earth, just about, to take a vacation here. It was the grand and public testimonial of the mother planet's achievement in establishing the web of interstellar linkages. That kilometre-square block was a replica of Platt's World; in basement bars you could eat crisp sticks of peppertree and wash away the tingling after-taste with minty cordials, while skirling pipe-music like a gale in treetops made your head ring. Over there was a compound imitating Shialongtwi, where to the accompaniment of solemn gongs the people paraded with enormous coloured flags whose symbolism recounted the history of their ancestors' struggles to tame and civilise an alien world. Down by the seashore were the wide-spaced houses typical of Glory, where tonight as usual they would dance on the grass and toss prickaburrs at one another's clothing, and those who did not want to be caught and partnered would remember that the burrs would not stick on skin. Glory was sometimes fun. Maybe she ought to invite Thorkild to go there with her one night. It could breach the wall that seemed to have built itself between them. And it was bad for this to happen when people were obliged to work so closely together.

Why had he not returned her call?

Effortfully she tore away her gaze from the window. There was no need for her to look at reality to see the city; a computer-generated three-dimensional model of it was projected within the transparent depths of the table around which the committee was seated. It also incorporated their agenda, by projecting little coloured stars varying from red to pale blue according to estimated order of importance on the areas relating to matters they intended to consider. Today was unusual; there were two stars floating in mid-air, indicative of the aspirant worlds not yet represented in the Bridge City.

So . . . first things first. She said to Metchel, of the Ways and Means Department, "Are we going to have to make any major re-allotment of ground-space?"

"Not for quite a while," Metchel answered, showing over-large front teeth in a rabbity smile. "We can trim the Kayowa section as soon as the current emigration programme is fulfilled; that's in three or four months. That should suffice for Ipewell, which I gather is extremely backward, unless there's a sudden renewed fad for the primitive, and the computer analyses show no sign of one."

Once again: evidence that human beings were coming to fit the measure of their machines. Alida sighed and made a note by subvocalising to her personal computer.

"What about Azrael, though?"

"Well, we shan't know until we get Chen's report, shall we?"

Bella Soong of the Adaptive Ecology Department leaned forward.

"Chen? Jacob Chen? Is he on Azrael? They must have run into trouble if they sent for him!"

It was on the tip of Alida's tongue to ask why she hadn't heard the news already. Then she recalled that it had been so long since any new colonised worlds were discovered that Bella had been on pre-retirement sabbatical. Only the unprecedented encounter with two aspirant worlds at once had led to her being recalled because her deputy was still incompletely qualified.

She said, "The captain of the scoutship asked for him. Her regular pantologist had handled the Bridge programme okay, but when it came to the cultural analysis he couldn't cope."

"In that case I think we should proceed with at least the preliminary arrangements for an Azrael section in Bridge City," Bella said. "Knowing Jacob as I do, I assume we'll have his results before we're ready to digest them if we don't make some sort of preparations."

Alida gazed down into the table, thinking of the clash of cultures, the different dialects, the weird mores—the religions, even, archaic though that notion was—which the existence of the Bridge System had wished on fat, lazy, complacent Earth. Now and then within Bridge City there were even fights, invariably due to misunderstanding, invariably apologised for . . . but sometimes there were injuries, and there had even been a death or two since she took office, and of those she was peculiarly ashamed.

She slapped the table-top, open-palmed.

"No, we dare not raise people's expectations ahead of time. I grant that Jacob Chen's a genius, but if they had to send for him that implies they found something exceptionally difficult. Ipewell looks like a good plain case, so we can carry on with that one. Later on I'll have a word with Moses van Heemskirk and report back. Now what else . . . ?" She scanned the model; the reddest star remaining was over the Riger's World zone, and it was coded for Laverne, the psychologist in charge of mores adjustment, a too-clever man with an insincere smile which he wore even in bed.

Why was she becoming so cynical? Alida shivered. The machines disagreed with her, and certainly since being appointed he had run his department as efficiently as could be wished. She repressed her momentary distaste.

"Laverne! You have a headache, apparently?"

The metaphor provoked his smile, as usual. "Yes, a preacher from Riger's, name of Rungley. You know about him?"

"The snake-handler? Of course."

"They let him loose this morning on Thorkild's instructions. Koriot Angoss assured him this would be okay. But whereas on Riger's he's merely a member of a fanatical minority sect, he's a novelty here, and a nuisance."

"How?"

"Angoss's idea was that he should be given some deadly snakes, wind up in hospital, and go home in embarrassment. Only the results of his quarantine examination showed that he has the enzyme S-herpetinase. A black mamba could spit in his eye and he'd just wipe away the tears."

Alida tensed. "You mean he's immune?"

"As a log of wood. The enzyme has been selected for among his ancestors, on a chance basis for who-knows-how-many generations, and since emigration to Riger's, deliberately. He has it from both sides of his family."

"What do you foresee?"

"I'll pipe you the full computation. But in essence what I'm afraid of is that bored young daredevils will attempt to imitate his feats, and people who don't have the enzyme will require a lot of intensive chemotherapy. We might even lose a life or two, and I don't have to spell out what will happen in that case, do I?"

Indeed not! But while Alida was still trying to find something more constructive to put into words than her annoyance with Thorkild, who should have delayed his decision until the quarantine report was through, the solido projector on the far side of the office uttered its shrill priority signal. They all turned, to see Responsible van Heemskirk's image appear. He wore an ill-tempered expression, and patches of sweat were darkening his robe.

An extraordinary sense of unreasoning excitement gripped Alida. Never before had she seen this suave politician in such a state of agitation. And his voice corresponded.

"Have you been discussing Azrael?" he barked.

"Yes, of course!" she answered. "Not in detail, but—"

"You wasted your time. There weren't any details to speak of until now. You know we sent Jacob Chen there to sort out the social analysis? Well, he got caught up in some local ritual."

"And they killed him."

All their eyes fastened in horror on van Heemskirk's round face, gleaming with perspiration.

"And what's more!" he pursued. "We've had to put Jorgen Thorkild under sedation. He's had a breakdown and insulted the representative from Ipewell, and the System feels as though it's grinding to a halt."

There was a dead pause. At length Alida rose.

"I guess I'd better abort this meeting and come see you," she said.

"Yes, it's nothing one should discuss remotely. And bring Laverne with you. Any planet with mores that result in the murder of a top pantologist is going to require exceptional adjustment!"

A tall woman wearing scarlet uniform was physically present in van Heemskirk's office, her face as still and noble as an ebony carving; she was introduced as Captain Lucy Inkoos, newly returned by Bridge from Azrael. Also present, but only in image—actually he was half around the world, in the Gobi Gardens—was Minister Shrigg. It was his task to liaise between the governors and the governed, to act as a spokesman before the public when there was any risk of the latter doubting the competence of the administrative élite. As Alida and Laverne arrived, he was saying loudly, "There will have to be an inquiry, of course!"

His tone was that of someone to whom official inquiries were the main business of life. And that was so. Earth, a single planet, had for half a millennium been too populous to be ruled in any traditional sense. It had to be run, like a machine of immense complexity, by dedicated experts. As for trying to govern *forty* planets—! No, the most that could be hoped for was that they would regard it as in their own best interests to co-operate in the scheme devised a century ago on Earth.

Passive but suspicious, the mass of humanity had to be constantly placated. Sometimes that meant resorting to the ancient practice of naming a scapegoat; sometimes it was enough to apologise for an error and accept that a lesson would be learned from it. But the death of a pantologist whose fame for decades had been inter-stellar . . .

Alida would not have cared to be in Shrigg's position. (Position? But they were present, and he was not . . . The constant paradox recurred! How could you

deal with a *real* problem if you yourself were absent?
Even given their chance to visit facsimiles of the
colony worlds at Bridge City, even granted that simply by applying for a number on the permanent open
list they could visit whichever other planet they
chose, did not in fact the citizens of Earth think of the
rest of the galaxy as inferior to the solido images in
their own homes?)

Well, maybe the shocking death of Jacob Chen . . .

She caught herself. Saxena's suicide should have
taught her better than to try and make death into a
positive event.

But Captain Inkoos was replying to Shrigg.

"The inquiry will tell you nothing that I can't.
Chen decided to take part in a deadly ritual. Local
custom permits them. Afterwards the victims are
avenged. We were invited to attend the execution."

Shrigg promptly put the kind of questions that the
public might be expected to frame.

"Was he intending to be killed?"

"I imagine he was gambling on getting away with
it."

"Hmm! A risky act, wouldn't you say? What about
your staff pantologist? Every scoutship has one,
right?"

"He failed to complete a social match-programme,
which would have enabled us to create a compatible
interface Earth-to-Azrael. On the grounds that he
wished to improve his cross-cultural competence he
applied for and was granted sabbatical leave, to be
spent travelling on all the inhabited planets. When I
filed a request for a replacement, I did not specify
Chen by name, and I was amazed when he arrived."

"Was it you who approved this arrangement,
Moses?" Shrigg demanded.

"Chen was in need of a challenge," van Heemskirk

replied. "It was his decision, not mine. I merely drew the problem to his attention. You know what pantologists are like. I was naturally glad when he consented."

Shrigg gnawed his lower lip thoughtfully for a while. So far everything appeared to have been done in strict accordance with protocol. He said at length, "But we have representatives from Azrael right here on Earth, don't we? Negotiating the regular Bridge System contract?"

"Of course!" van Heemskirk said promptly.

"And we dare not enter into such a contract without a total comprehension of their way of life. I put it to you that the first priority is to create our interface. But which if any of our *surviving* pantologists would accept the assignment? Laverne?"

The psychologist appeared to have anticipated the inquiry. With all the confidence he could draw from his computers by subvocal communication, he said, "Ask Hans Demetrios. He's very young, but he's shown exceptional promise. Currently he's at Ipewell, and I'm informed that he grew so bored after the preliminary contact stages that he wrote a programme for the Ipewell Bridge just to keep himself amused. It checked out flawlessly. What do you think?"

"Well, I guess it makes good sense not to risk another of our *advanced* pantologists," Shrigg said, and in his ironical acceptance could be heard all the cynicism of the billions whom he represented, who had to take their experience of interstellar travel at second hand not because their government had decreed it but because there wasn't time to let everybody visit every human world, or even spend a vacation at Bridge City.

Relieved that the argument had not been more protracted, Alida was able to pick up the point which interested her most.

"Did you say Jorgen had a breakdown? When? And why?"

"It appeared as though," said van Heemskirk deliberately, "it was triggered off by the delegate from Azrael, Lancaster Long."

VI

———————————

"Where are you going, Hans?"

As soon as he had time, Hans Demetrios looked up. The sliding panel which closed the doorway of his cabin had crept ajar, and there was only one member of the ship's crew to whom he had accorded authority to intrude on his privacy: Fay Logan. Her face appeared in the opening, lips parted and shiny-moist, eyes narrowed but very bright.

"Come in!" he invited, and added: "Back to Earth. They sent for me."

"Earth!" She was taken aback. Her eyes darted over the disarray as she entered the room; the cabinets were emptying themselves according to programme, clothing this way, tools that, microbooks into tidy cartons. Even the ship's library, designed to cope with the needs of over a hundred crewfolk, could not satisfy the information-hunger of a pantologist, so Hans travelled with his own. It was cheaper than re-activating a Bridge whenever he grew bored.

But she knew all about his capacity for boredom.

She closed the panel and leaned against it.

"You didn't tell me you were leaving Ipewell!"

"It only just happened. I'm sorry."

Staring at him as he folded his favourite microbook reader and tucked it into the appropriate package, Fay thought: yes, he is sorry. He means it. But that doesn't mean he's sorry for not telling me—rather, he's sorry it didn't occur to him to tell me. He never gives enough weight to the possibility that other people's lives might be as important as his own.

"How long ago?" she challenged.

"Oh—not more than an hour, I guess."

"And you're set to leave already. It must be very urgent!" She could not prevent her tone from sounding sarcastic.

"Well, kind of urgent, I guess. But after all I am finished on Ipewell. The culture-interface is ready; the Bridge programme is ready; what else is there? It was all rather easy because the population is small and homogeneous."

Small? There are scores of millions of people here! Even if the people aren't counted by the billions, as Earth's are, surely—

But a pantologist's universe could not be the same as hers—or she would be one!

For the first time it crossed her mind how terrible it might be to inhabit a cosmos where people were as anonymous, interchangeable, and ultimately dull as the computers must find them when wrapping and packaging them for interstellar transit. Hans had been tender to her, affectionate, physically attentive; there had remained a barrier on the mental level which in this moment she knew she was destined never to breach.

She said dully, "I see. So what are you going to do next?"

"They killed Jacob Chen on Azrael when he was trying to get to grips with the dynamic of the local culture. They're sending me to finish his work. It's a great honour." He finished storing the microbooks and began double-checking what the machinery had done with his recording crystals.

Fay closed her eyes for a moment. On the interior of her eyelids she seemed to see herself reflected as others would see her: indisputably lovely, with flawlessly tanned skin, an excellently proportioned figure, violet eyes that contrasted admirably with her curly fair hair . . . Hans had said what other men had said, in his own detached weighing-the-evidence fashion which somehow made the statement that much more sincere and precious. He had said, "You are beautiful, you know." And so, she had thought, was he!

But now when she looked at him again she realised he was according her no attention beyond the minimum that anyone deserved.

She tried one last time to engage his full attention. Touching his arm, she said, "Hans—look at me!"

Before he smiled his answer, though, he had to prepare himself as she had often seen him do before when arguing with the computers: it is necessary for me to be distracted, and therefore I will do it, but out of duty, not from choice . . .

It had been in her mind to kiss him, cheeks and eyelids first, then fiercely on the mouth with the intention of reawakening what they had shared. She abandoned the idea, and contented herself with a mere peck.

He . . . tasted wrong.

"That," she improvised, "was sort of to say goodbye."

"Maybe it won't be goodbye." He gave her hand a comforting squeeze. "Don't assume they're going to kill me, too!"

The implied reproach recalled her to the real world. Like everyone else she knew, she was aware of Chen's status as a pantologist. He had been a pupil of the very first, a link with the original conception of the idea which had been elevated into an article of faith, the belief that there would always be humans who could out-argue their machines.

She ought to be told what had happened to draw Hans away.

"What went wrong?" she said at last, letting go his hand.

All the means which would have enabled him to project the details to her, using the ship's resources, had by now been stored in six neat cases. Rather than unpack them again, he recounted the story in bald words.

"I see," Fay said at last. "What appeals to you is being sent for to cope with a problem that killed Chen. All that matters in your life is another challenge, and preferably one that someone else has been defeated by."

"Oh, no!" was his immediate response. And then, as his permament curiosity set in again: "What makes you say so?"

"Oh, I worked it out the night we met the two boys, Lork and Jeckin," she said with a sigh. "You made it clearer to them what had happened to this culture than the rest of us had managed in a year when talking with the people in charge!"

"I can't help it!" Hans retorted in an injured tone. And then, as by way of extenuation: "I look at things differently, I'm afraid."

It was the most personal comment she had ever provoked from him. She smiled and gestured for him to continue.

"I can't help it!" he repeated, starting to pace up and down in the narrow confines of the room. "I don't know how true it is, the idea that the existence of computers has forced us into evolutionary hyperdrive, but it does fit, doesn't it? Someone has to stay in charge! I don't want to be overtaken by machinery!"

He drove fist into palm.

"It makes me terrified, you know—what I do, what I'm compelled to do! I have to argue with the medical computers whenever they run a check on the ship's personnel, because they don't understand what's driving me! My job engages everything, every single faculty, like clinging with fingers and toes to a sheer rock wall. You inch up, and every inch is an achievement, and one little slip is the end. Do you believe it's terrifying? Anyone else can fail and start over. A pantologist has to assume he got it right the first time. If it happened to me I'd stop being what I am, and that would be infinitely worse than—oh—being crippled in a wheelchair! Maybe Chen preferred death to failure; *I* don't know! All I *do* know is that *I* would!"

"So—" Fay ventured. He cut her short.

"Why should I do what I do? Oh, because I'm selfish, of course! Once you've succeeded for a while, you don't want to do anything that entails the risk of defeat. The strain itself becomes attractive. Nothing else uses so much of you! And it earns you admiration, and that's not enough to repay your efforts, and then sometimes you get a bonus. And you saw me get one. That is enough."

Confused, she said, "Are you still talking about Lork and Jeckin?"

"What else? They're going to be liberated. I know! I analysed this culture, broke it down into symbols, weighted them, stored them in the memory-banks, told the computers where they were misunderstanding me, ran tests for interaction with Earth and the other planets in the Bridge System . . . This culture is sterile. It's going to collapse. I've fed the hunger in those kids' eyes! Didn't you *see* it?"

"Yes"—barely breathing the word.

"When they build the Ipewell Bridge, the engineers will be instructed by the computers. But I taught the computers what to say. I set those boys free."

Seeming suddenly embarrassed at having talked so openly, Hans ceased his pacing. "I guess I have to make a move. They have to fire up an Earthside Bridge for me specially, and I don't want them to waste any power. I'm sorry, Fay."

"For what?" she riposted, and then, not giving him time to answer, continued: "Tell me something before you go. Jacob Chen must have been sixty-plus, right?"

"Sixty-two."

"And he'd been a pantologist all his life?"

Hans blinked. "Well, I guess so. We tend to be infant prodigies as often as not."

"When did you find out you were going to be one?"

"I didn't. Other people found out for me. I was just about learning to read when they latched on."

"And you were how old then?"

"Oh!" He gave a boyish and self-conscious grin. "Not quite past my third birthday."

"So I'm half a century too late to try and catch up," she said, and gave a bitter smile. "Never mind. I'll console myself with the certainty that I shan't be the last person to break her heart by setting it on you. I just hope there will go on being enough to save you from . . ."

The words died away, and there he was blinking at her, genuinely not understanding: this man who understood almost literally everything else.

To have achieved this petty triumph against a pantologist's universal brilliance did not strike Fay as any sort of fair compensation for her distress. But it was what she was going to have to make do with.

"Plugging in for Earth in one minute," said the unemotional voice of a recording filtered by the PA system. "Wait for the green light, please."

When it showed, Hans gave his baggage the necessary tap to align it on its nulgrav carrier and followed it across the painted line on the floor which defined the transit zone.

During the seconds which remained before his own journey, he thought about how this modern miracle must have affected Mother Uskia and her companions when they went to Mars. A Bridge was simple enough in principle. It relied on the fact that any given volume of space differed from any other only to the extent that it was distorted by the presence of nearby matter and a flow of energy passing through it. Cancel those differences, and anywhere might as well be anywhere else. Because all humanly habitable planets were about the same size and orbited roughly the same kind of sun, it wasn't hard to reduce the distinctions to an effective null state. Then, to specify a particular destination, it was enough to introduce another, planned, difference.

At the mark, obedient machines did precisely that, and the recorded voice invited Hans to walk into a volume of space identical with one on Earth. It *was* on Earth. It had cost a hundred gigawatts of power per kilogram of transferred mass to maintain the identity of the two spaces during transmission, and the computers keeping unbroken watch over that identity would have noted, reacted to and cancelled out about ten to the eighth information-bits corresponding to incipient discrepancies.

And he, Hans Demetrios, had taught the computers what discrepancies to look out for.

He was very sorry for Fay. He wished with all his heart she could be more than just a charming, attractive, highly intelligent person.

But she wasn't.

It had been courteous of him to comply with her desires. Refusing her would have caused hurt. But in the long run she had been hurt anyway. The fact preyed on his mind. A pantologist wanted to know that people had benefited by his existence, not suffered by it. It was an article of faith to him that causing pain was inherently wrong, though naturally there were no more rational reasons for such a conclusion than there had been in the old days when people believed in religions, with a god or gods all set to punish them for misbehaviour. Those beliefs hadn't saved the ancients from untold centuries of misery—war, slavery, villeinage, epidemics, droughts and famines . . . And no more could his creed prevent Hans from unintentionally making somebody like Fay unhappy.

Recognising the fact, however, did little to cheer him up. One day, though, he promised himself: one day he would no longer make that sort of mistake!

He was relieved to find someone rising to greet him at the receptor end of the Bridge. And realised for the first time just how important was the mission he had been assigned. For the men came forward and extended his hand. He was physically present, whereas a solido would have been more usual.

After exchanging courtesies, he went on, "It's local night down here, so you won't be pitchforked into your new problem straight away. I've arranged accommodation for you in the Bridge Centre, and all the data you need to study will be piped to your suite. Tomorrow at ten hundred you're to meet with the Supervisor of Relations, Alida Marquis—in person at her office, if you've no objection."

As they grew older and more remote, some pantologists did, Hans was aware, develop a reluctance to meet anybody face to face. But it hadn't—obviously—overtaken Chen, and he was in some senses the greatest of them all.

He said, "That'll be fine by me. But—ah—just one thing."

"Yes?" The other cocked his head alertly.

"Will there be a funeral, or a memorial service, or anything, for Jacob Chen? I'd like to be there."

"Under the circumstances . . . no."

"What circumstances?"

"He recorded a will, just before he left the *Hunting Dog* to go for his final walk on Azrael. He ordered that if he failed in his assignment—which was to be taken for granted if he did not come back to wipe the recording—his body was to be cremated without ceremony and no memorial was to be erected to him. It has been decided that his wish must be complied with."

A shiver crawled down Hans's spine. Moments ago he had been proud that they had picked him to take over where Chen quit; now, all of a sudden, he was terribly afraid.

VII

Sometimes in dreams, when she was much younger, Alida had seen the Bridge System as a fountain of rainbows. In Norse legend there was a rainbow bridge: Bifrost, which heroes crossed to gain Valhalla. Little by little such dreams had receded, like the moving of the real rainbow, always in the next field, over the next fence, until it faded away.

Had Saxena gone to the place of heroes, he who had yielded to the temptation of poison?

Despondent, she wandered through the polyplanet city which had originated between a low range of hills and an ocean, then overflowed on to artificial islands. Here the people of all the human worlds could come together and pretend that as well as being cousins they were friends. It had been laid out on the assumption that there would be a constant outward flow of Earthsiders to the other planets, more or less balancing the flood of those who came as tourists to the mother planet. But the effort it was costing to maintain that balance . . . ! True, the outworld visitors generally stayed only a month or so, and very few applied to settle and only three per cent made a second trip, because if they could spare the time—money was no object—they preferred to take in a full cross-section of humanity's settlements. All to the good, of course, as Laverne was forever pointing out, because the daughter planets must also be kept in contact with each other . . .

Even so: it was a constant struggle to make any significant portion of Earth's population go anywhere, be it for a mere vacation. Filling the emigrant quotes for Kayowa and Platt's World, forty thousand each, was taking as long as the computers had predicted, despite an advertising campaign designed to attract a rush of volunteers. Privately she had been expecting the machines, for once, to be proven wrong. They had been, more than once, when she was younger; obviously they had made progress while human beings stayed where they were. (Stayed where they were! In the epoch when Bridges linked the stars, why did the folk of Earth no longer look up at them?)

Maybe because tonight at Glory there was nothing happening to speak of: just the professional entertainers going through the motions, and a few elderly tourists. A whisper had soughed among the variegated buildings, and people were following it like dead leaves following the wind, searching for the rumoured newest-latest.

Going with them, wearing a golden mask and nothing else bar a cloak and sandals which, had she remained at Glory, she would have discarded an hour ago, Alida felt her mind cycle over and over like an old-fashioned spaceship distress call. Usually when she passed through the microcosm she was responsible for, saw all the contrasting costumes and heard the multifarious accents ringing in her ears, she was exhilarated. Tonight she felt a lowering sensation of depression and decay, as though a dank warm mist had closed invisibly on the land.

Thorkild had suffered a breakdown. Because she

had been told about that, on each of the sectors of Bridge City she could sense, almost see, a thing like a monstrous hoof crushing down: as against a rainbow, the fog-brown drabness of a real Bridge.

Thorkild had suffered a breakdown. She did not like him very much, but she was obliged to respect him, and in a sense whoever held the Directorship of the Bridge System symbolised Earth's grandest achievement. Was it to crumble because no one could be found to cope with an impossible task?

Thorkild had suffered a breakdown. Although he had well concealed it until the final moment, so had Saxena. And his predecessor had retired owing to the unbearable strain and died over-young, and the person before her, and before him again, back to when there were only a dozen worlds in the System.

To relate even that many planets in any constructive way was a task for the gods, or for heroes, and the gods were dead and the heroes all gone across the rainbow, and that left men and women. There were the handful (out of the whole species, how many thousand?) who could out-reason a computer over the span of a million-word program; of them, there were a few score who could define a planetary culture so that mindless machines could understand it. And then there were the people—nearly as few—who could use the tools the computers thereupon gave them. She was one. Jorgen was another. So was Laverne. Moses, too, for all his politician's mannerisms: he was of the clan, whereas Shrigg was not, and made it plain that he resented the fact.

Must everything ultimately devolve on a single person? Sometimes she suspected that might be so. She felt so lonely since losing Saxena . . .

But, as she realised with a start, she actually wasn't. The group she was absently following had swollen to a horde, thousands strong, converging on Riger's, where some of the plants had pink leaves and all the buildings were faced with a reddish resilient wood. She recognised how dense the throng must be because it was so rare for the computers to activate the crowd-control mechanisms which were among the few non-authentic aspects of these outworld-replica zones. The Earthsiders reacted automatically to the signal-lamps and the polite automatic requests which burred through the air; now and then she caught a snatch of conversation as someone explained to an off-world visitor what he or she was supposed to do in response.

One ought probably to be proud of the fact that Earthsiders could now be in a crowd and not turn into a mob, thought Alida. But what else would one expect of those who bothered to come here? They, if anyone, must be admirers of the Bridge System. They must comprehend the problems that it posed . . .

Did they? Did they realise how it had avalanched into existence the people who though they had incredible power were no longer as free as those beneath them—who did the work because the job was there, who had to undertake it because there was no one else who could?

If so, why were so many of them gathering together to watch a preacher being bitten by a snake?

The most discomfortable word in any language, Alida said to herself, must be *conscience*. It had pursued Jacob Chen beyond the gates of death; she was still inclined to shiver when she remembered the intensity with which he had declared his last will to the camera. Shrigg might hold all the inquiries he liked, as a man turns up wet stones to watch grubs writhe in the unfamiliar light of day. None, though they were to last a million years, could expose and define the soul of somebody like Chen.

By now the crowd she was pressed among was overflowing the rim of the artificial amphitheatre at the heart of the Riger's World section of the city. On every side people were laughing and joking, passing polychrome containers of liquor, offering other more exotic drugs from a dozen worlds to be swallowed or inhaled or rubbed into the mucous membranes. In the jostling mêlée she felt a man come close, and a hand inquired under her cloak. It would be meant as flattery, and had she stayed at Glory she would have taken it as such. But here and now everything felt wrong. She tilted back her mask and gazed at the masked face of him who had touched her, and he met her eyes and hastened away.

It occurred to her that she would not have liked to confront a mirror wearing the look she must have bestowed on him.

Suddenly disgusted with herself and the pressure of so many people, because it was too like the actualisation of the illusion she had suffered all evening long—the Bridge System as a suffocating brown hoof of fog—she thrust at random among the crowd. She must have exuded some sort of authority; to her surprise she found herself isolated, moments later, at a prime position: atop a little knoll three or four metres wide, commanding a splendid view of the stage downslope.

People were crammed together, kneeling, sitting or lolling over the whole of the rest of the grassy ground. Why then should she be privileged—?

Ah: but she was not alone. Standing in front of her was one extremely tall man in a high fur hat and a sweeping robe of blue embroidered with silver thread.

Even by his back she recognised him, from the solido recordings she had played. He was the leader of the Azrael delegation, Lancaster Long.

The shock was fearful. Alida had not yet braced

herself to meet anybody from the deadly world
which had cost Chen his life. The encounter was to
be pre-arranged, maybe in a week or so, when Moses
van Heemskirk had finished the briefing stage and
serious negotiations were under way.

But, at least, he had not noticed her. She was
minded to sidle away, when she realised why he was
staring down towards the stage with such intensity.
The next show was due to begin. And those who had
not thought to bring magnifiers—for this amphitheatre, being a duplicate of one on Riger's, was not
equipped with air-lenses or even TV remotes—were
bound to rely on unaided vision. She was not going to
get such a good view from anywhere else.

Accordingly she remained, and even took a pace
closer to him.

On stage appeared a man in a brown shirt and loose
brown breeches. He took station at the foot of a
gilded caduceus twice as high as himself, the eyes of
its twined snakes glowing baleful red. Obviously this
must be Rungley. He had an untidy light-brown
beard and a thick mop of unkempt hair. Behind and
to either side stood a choir of children singing in edgy
shrill voices. The tune was catchy and rhythmical,
though she could not make out the worlds; still, she
did not need to. *A priori* it must have to do with the
legend she had learned about from the tapes she had
played during the past few days. Rungley's cult was
less religious than nationalist, even though religions
still existed on Riger's World; each ceremony was a
re-enactment of the way their forefathers had overcome the originally dominant species on their new
planet, a quasi-reptilian beast which by coincidence
expelled jets of poison from its forward end.

Later, when contact with Earth was re-established,
computers had worked out that in a million years or
so that species could well have evolved into intelli-

gence. The same was true for at least five other planets where humans were now dominant. Maybe there was a burden of guilt on the collective soul of Earth which could account for this monstrous depression Alida and so many others were feeling . . .

But there was never any way of undoing the past. One had to make do with what there was. Perhaps eventually the pantologists would give rise to a more civilised version of humanity—except that most of them cared little about passing on their genes, lived solitary lives whether male or female . . .

Was the cream of the race heading down a dead end?

Close to the stage, staring up at Rungley, were a group of men and women in dark clothing, comfortably seated as though they had taken station well ahead of time. She thought she recognised—though the light was poor—members of the resident staff from Riger's, come to see what their fellow-citizen was up to. Some small argument was going on.

It ended, and a box was handed up from behind them, with gingerly care. Rungley took it in one brawny hand and with the other slapped the lid open. Reaching inside, he produced a long and squirming snake.

With part of her mind Alida reflected how amazing was the effect such a creature could have on an audience like this, most of whom could never have seen one except in a solido recording. Gawking at animals in cages had ceased to be popular centuries ago; what zoos remained were for educational purposes and research, and access to the wild conservation zones was even more strictly regulated.

Yet here were modern humans reacting in the way that, primitive scientific accounts reported, their extinct cousins like chimpanzees and gorillas would have done: cringing at the mere shape of it . . .

A solid wave of silence seemed to pass through the assembled multitude, like a phonon zone in super-cooled helium.

Rungley bent forward, letting fall the box, and thrust his thick tongue between his teeth. The snake struck.

By the fangs sunk in his tongue, he drew its head into his mouth. And bit.

And spat the dead head to the floor, along with a reddish spray of saliva mixed with blood.

There was an awed pause, punctuated by screams. Then came a thunder of applause, and yells of, "More! *More!*"

Alida stood transfixed, almost deafened by the pounding in her ears. Even when a voice she recognised spoke close to her she could not tear her gaze away. She said only, "What do you want?"

It was Koriot Angoss. And he answered, "To know what I did wrong! I spotted you on the monitor cameras, and I was sure you couldn't be here by chance—"

"I am!" she interrupted. "I swear it! Yes, I am!"

"But *why?*" Angoss moaned. "Rungley's a cheap mountebank! He's planted snakes among the crowd so he can do what you just saw, and it's a trick that Persian conjurers used to do in pre-atomic times, and on Riger's we find it too disgusting to be entertaining. And I thought Earthsiders were past the stage where killing animals was thought amusing! Can't you invoke a conservation law? Even if he brought his own snakes?"

"You told Jorgen he was safe to be let loose!" Alida countered, turning at last to face Angoss.

"But I didn't realise he was going to pull this trick as a crowd-pleaser! Importing snakes can affect the ecology—why didn't Bella Soong file a complaint?

And if people on Earth no longer enjoy killing for its own sake, *why are they cheering*?"

Alida made to cobble together excuses, more for her colleagues' sake than her own, but was interrupted. The hawk-faced man in the blue robe had turned to them.

He said, "This fellow Rungley—one of you is from his home world?"

"I am!" Angoss admitted.

"I present myself: Lancaster Long of the planet Azrael. I have been watching this preacher since his show commenced. We do not have snakes on Azrael, but my understanding is that they can sometimes be venomous, and I have seen him bitten three or four times without exhibiting any ill effects. Has he selected non-venomous species, and if so, what is there of interest in his performance?"

"They aren't non-venomous," said Alida; her tongue felt almost too thick to articulate her words. "But he's immune."

A glare of distaste crossed Long's regal features.

"Does he know it?"

"Oh, sure!" said Angoss bitterly. "Do you imagine he'd take the risk if he weren't?"

"I see!" Long spoke in a tone like winter wind. "I had hoped that here for once was a person who took life seriously. Instead, it turns out he's a cynical trickster, and people are glad to be deluded by him. It's of a piece with everything I've seen since I was inveigled into coming here."

Nettled by his scornful manner, Alida said, "Explain!"

"Why do you need an explanation? A man is not poisoned by water; would you go to see a man drink water? That is how you have persuaded me to waste my time!" Sweeping his robe around him, he strode off down the slope. Such was his air of command, people moved aside automatically.

"Who's that?" Angoss demanded. Alida told him that she knew of Long and his background in a few short sentences, admiring against her will the way in which people were making way for him as though by the same kind of reflex that dictated their reaction to Rungley's snakes.

Angoss got the point before she did, and with a wordless cry started out in Long's wake. Even then she stood wondering and foolish for a moment before she too understood and hastened down the little hill.

By the time they attained the stage—people not making way for them as they had for Long—it was too late to interfere. Where all the snakes had come from, Alida didn't waste time guessing; any computer could no doubt have told her, but nobody had thought to ask the proper question, any more than they had remembered to inquire whether Rungley had the special enzyme which protected him. One could only ask the right questions when one knew most of the answer . . .

At all events Long had beaten her and Angoss to the showdown.

He had arrived at the stage just as yet another magnificent reptile was being passed up for the preacher to play with: a full-grown rattlesnake, its tail louder than its mouth.

And snatched hold of it. His scorn was magnificent, too. He towered over Rungley, and the preacher quailed as the snake was swung dangling before his face.

"This is not a man!" Long cried at the top of his voice. "Your Rungley is a charlatan! He knows he is immune to venom! He risks nothing when he allows a snake to strike him! His actions are a lie and a sham!"

A swell of grumbling complaint at having their fun

interrupted disturbed the crowd. He quelled it with a lordly scowl, the snake still hanging from his grasp like the whips which on his world had preceded the death of Jacob Chen.

"I," Long said, "do *not* know whether I'm immune. See *this*!"

And he shook his left arm bare of his loose sleeve and offered it to the ready fangs.

VIII

Arriving in her office next morning after a sleepless night, Alida was for a long while unable to settle to work. Instead she paced around and around the table with the model city projected beneath its surface, powerless to take her eyes off the representation of Riger's. Memory kept replaying for her last night's events in the amphitheatre: the near-panic among the crowd, the arrival of the flying ambulance to carry off Long, the insistence of a handful of trouble-makers that Rungley continue with his act . . . which, on realising how they regarded him, he had refused to do.

And that had come close to triggering a riot.

Damn Angoss for regarding Rungley so lightly! He had apologised over and over, but what use were apologies now? And damn Jorgen too, for having been content to accept the advice of an outworlder instead of doing what he was supposed to: rely on his own judgment.

Eventually she gave a sudden bitter chuckle and turned to the controls which projected captions and symbols upon the image of the city. A few moments' work supplied seven words in luminous red letters.

They read: WHY IS A MOUSE WHEN IT SPINS?

After a while the answer didn't seem funny any more.

She compelled herself to sit down at her desk. Not long remained before ten hundred, when Hans Demetrios was due, but she ought at least to call the hospital where they had taken Thorkild. She gave the desk the necessary instructions.

"What's the chief therapist's name?" she added.

"Dr Lorenzo," came the sweetly-inflected answer, and she tensed in dismay. How could she not have known? He had given expert evidence at the inquest following Saxena's suicide; not only had they met face to face but she had taken up an hour of his time afterwards, pestering him for more and better explanations. Later, in the grip of depression, she had thought of consulting him about it, but never quite been driven to that extreme.

Nonetheless, she should not have forgotten he was in charge of that of all the hospitals in the hemisphere . . .

The desk reported that Lorenzo was out of range of a solido circuit but could talk to her on a sound-only connection; would that do? Really, this automatic courtesy sometimes went too far! She snapped a yes, and was instantly annoyed with herself; there was nothing more pointless than losing one's temper with a machine.

Almost at once the familiar voice rang out: deep and professionally reassuring.

"Alida! Let me start by saying how sorry I am that we should renew contact under these unhappy circumstances! I take it you are inquiring after Jorgen?"

"Yes, of course. Have you made a diagnosis?"

"Only a tentative one, I'm afraid. I've scarcely had

a chance to talk to him since he emerged from sedation, but the pattern, at least, is indicative."

"What does it point to?"

"A not uncommon phenomenon. Though that doesn't mean it's going to be any easier to treat. Are you familiar with the term acedia?"

Alida hesitated. At length she said, "I'm afraid I'm not well grounded in psychiatric terminology."

"Oh, it far pre-dates the emergence of psychological medicine as an independent discipline." The tone of Lorenzo's words was such that Alida could picture the faintly patronising smile which must be on their speaker's face, and once again she trembled on the brink of rage. "Originally it was a theological concept: sloth, one of the seven deadly sins. Sin . . . ?"

"Yes, I know what that means."

"You'd be surprised how many people nowadays do not! And a good thing too, in my view. My patients seem to pick up quite enough burden of guilt in the natural course of their lives without being told that it's all inevitable because a jealous deity wished it on their ancestors. Still, as a referent I find this particular notion useful. Back in late medieval times it became more sophisticated, and was ultimately transformed into what was often called 'the black night of the soul'—a condition in which one questioned whether existence had any point at all. Naturally this was heretical because the faithful were required to accept *a priori* that the creation had a purpose even if the creatures could not comprehend it. I speak of a Christian tradition, you realise, which proved excessively infectious. Other religions managed to escape this particular trap."

Alida said slowly, "Jorgen's ancestors were Christians, weren't they?"

"Yes indeed. And, if you'll pardon my remarking on the fact, so were those of virtually everyone in a position of high authority at present. So were Saxena's, and your own."

He waited a moment, as though to let her react if she wanted to. But she said nothing.

"Not," he resumed, "that such an influence is essential to the onset of the condition. Within the past couple of decades cases of it have been reported on every continent. The relative fatalism of most other traditions acts as a protective barrier, but that's by no means a universal guarantee of immunity. An excess of gratification—a lack of challenge—any of several quite minor physiological imbalances affecting the central nervous system—oh, at least a score of stimuli can bring it about in a vulnerable personality. Like fever, it's one of a rather limited number of available responses which may be provoked by a wide range of inputs."

With a trace of impatience Alida said, "Thank you for the lecture! But have you forgotten what my discipline is?"

"Forgive me! The fault must be mine, for using this particular label with its specialised associations, instead of saying casually—as so many of my colleagues would—that he has sprained his mind. Possibly the physiological analogy is more apt. Even a trained athlete, with muscles in tip-top condition, is vulnerable to a sudden unexpected wrench, as when turning an ankle on a pebble that rolls from under foot. So with the trained mind."

"Something that Lancaster Long said?" Alida offered.

"How did you know that? Have you talked to him since the event? When?"

"No, of course not! But Moses van Heemskirk was there when it all started, and he told me."

And, her mind ran on, last night at Riger's I would have challenged Long concerning what he'd said—except that he preferred to be bitten by a rattlesnake . . .

"I see." She could practically hear Lorenzo biting his lip as he made inaudible notes. "Well, as I said, it's far too early for a diagnosis, really, let alone a prognosis. But I assure you we shall all do our best. And I promise to keep you in touch."

"I hope you can get him back to us soon. You know that for the first time ever we have two aspirant worlds to negotiate with simultaneously. And attempting to function without a Director of the System—"

"We'll do our best," Lorenzo repeated, and cut the circuit.

Alida sighed. Strictly, it had been unfair of her to press him so early in the case. But if she didn't know what was happening to Jorgen—

Abruptly she realised that in fact she didn't know much of what was going on anywhere; so far today she had neglected to check the news. She ordered her desk to present items of immediate interest in headline form with backup summaries, and with a trace of relief found almost all of what she read on the screen matching her expectations. The inquiry into Chen's death was under way. The delegate from Azrael was in hospital and Rungley had explained his collapse as due to lack of faith in . . . well, whatever the preacher had faith in: *S*-herpetinase, presumably. Koriot Angoss had made a preliminary statement. Negotiations for an Ipewell Bridge were to proceed as scheduled. Those for an Azrael Bridge were being temporarily postponed pending the verdict on Chen—

"But Shrigg doesn't have any right to do that!" Alida exclaimed aloud, reaching for an outside call-switch. In mid-movement she froze. She had had the sudden crazy impression she was looking at a dead man.

Then the illusion passed. The desk was relaying the

image of Hans Demetrios to inform her that he had arrived in the outer office, and the only resemblance was in his look—an inquiring, hungry look which Chen had also worn.

She had never seen it on anyone's face except a pantologist's.

"Send him in," she said wearily, and walked around the desk to greet him.

Shaking hands with her, he nodded at the sign she had inscribed in the depths of the table.

"I see your point," he said.

Gesturing him to a chair, she countered, "What do you mean?"

"The answer to your question, of course. Isn't it 'the higher, the fewer'?"

A smile came unbidden to her face. "That's right! I hadn't expected you to know. I hadn't expected many people at all to know. It must be a very old bit of nonsense."

"Twentieth century. And frankly I'm surprised you knew of it. But it is true, isn't it?"

She said in a dull voice, "So true that sometimes I find it terrifying."

He signified agreement with a nod. After that for a while they sat and looked at one another. Gradually Alida felt her sense of despondency leaving her. To know the answer to that ancient question, and to understand why she had been driven to make it her motto, was more than she would have expected from Thorkild, Saxena, anyone else she had ever met. Previously, when she had spoken with Hans, she had taken him for just another pantologist—in other words, someone who was fated to follow a particular route through life, blazed for him by his predecessors and constrained by the demands of the tasks that only a pantologist could undertake. Maybe the age which she concealed so well was getting the better of her. Meeting him again, like this, conveyed to her a powerful sense of his individuality, as though something were winding up behind his eyes to strike at her like a snake—*Stop!* She must rid herself of the images bequeathed to her by Rungley!

Rungley?

No: by Lancaster Long.

Hastily she said, "You're bound to go far higher than I ever shall. I wonder whether I should envy you."

"What's to envy? We're the unfreest of the unfree." He gave a shrug: since it couldn't be helped . . . "But you didn't invite me here to talk about myself. Is it about Azrael?"

With an effort she herded her thoughts back into their normal course.

"Yes, and there's an additional complication. You saw the news about Minister Shrigg ordering postponement of the Bridge negotiations?"

"Yes."

"What do you think of that?"

"I imagine he had no alternative."

"But access to the Bridge System is the right and privilege of any human world! It can't and mustn't be withheld!"

Hans refrained from answering directly. Instead he said, "I was watching the news last night when the first report came over about the Azrael delegate allowing the snake to bite him. You were actually present, weren't you?"

"Yes!"

"Do you know why he did it?"

"I . . ." She passed her fingers through her hair, looking away. "No. Do you?"

She had meant the question to be ironical; he took it at face value.

"My study of the material furnished on arrival permits a guess. He did it because he didn't know if the bite could kill him."

Alida revolved the words in her mind, hoping they would become clearer if she examined them from different angles. They didn't. At length she shook her head.

"How's Director Thorkild?" Hans said.

"I . . . why do you suddenly change the subject?"

"I haven't changed the subject."

A huge half-formed terror shadowy at the back of her mind, Alida struggled to make sense of this remark, too, and came closer. But the sense was worse than the shadow. She said, "I called the hospital and spoke with the chief therapist. It's a Dr Lorenzo."

"And—?"

"He talked about one of the seven deadly sins."

"I see." Hans frowned, gazing into nowhere. "That would be acedia, presumably. Yes? I must interview Lorenzo . . . You know what Long said, at the Bridge Centre?"

"Moses van Heemskirk was there, and repeated it to me yesterday. But what does this have to do with . . . ? Oh. I see what you meant when you said you hadn't changed the subject. At least I think I do. I can't help hoping I'm wrong. Make it a little plainer if you can."

"I'll try." Frowning, he leaned back, gaze on the ceiling. "The higher, the fewer. Out where Thorkild is, where you are, worse still where Chen got to, there are very few of us indeed. I can feel inside myself a faint echo of how it will be when I reach that kind of level."

He did not, she noticed, say "if." He was describing the future he had taken for granted the whole of his life.

"It's compounded of loneliness, exhaustion, and the feeling that even though you're envied by other people you are also being used by them, because they can never know how much it costs you to sustain your efforts. So in the end their praise and gratitude must ring hollow. The only praise that counts becomes self-praise. And how long can any human being live on that? Only so long as he can persuade himself that this slaving work is going to be worthwhile. If you falter in that, or if you're driven—as I suspect Chen was driven—to the conviction that you're faltering for another reason, such as old age or impaired judgment, you break apart. Jorgen Thorkild broke. But he *was broken*. And we know who by. So I'm going to take a calculated gamble."

Alida felt very cold; she wanted to shiver, but could not because in fact the room was comfortably warm. She husked, "What is it?"

"I'm going to advance to standby status in my head a hypothesis whose implications terrify me. I hope I can maintain it at that level, without ever letting myself believe in it entirely, until enough evidence turns up to contradict it. How I can manage that, I simply don't yet know. I'll have to work it out as I go along. I never dreamed I'd have to deliberately prevent myself from accepting what my powers of reason tell me, but if I do convince myself and then someone else proves I'm wrong—well, I'm certain you must have met enough pantologists to realise what will become of me."

"What's the hypothesis?" Alida cried. She saw in dismay that his face was shining with sweat.

Was this the kind of agony Saxena had endured, lacking the strength of character that would allow him to admit it openly?

"I'm going to make the only assumption, as far as I can tell, which Jacob Chen did not permit himself." Hans's tone remained perfectly calm. "He could not entertain, even for a moment, what I suspect must be the truth: that the people of Azrael are prepared to endure what they regard as the burden of existence solely and exclusively because they imagine it is their duty to put an end to it."

"But they could just commit suicide!"

"That torment would be insufficient. Dedicated as they are to suffering, they build up so there will be something to destroy; they reproduce so there will be more to kill. There were millenniary sects of that kind here on Earth in the far past; most other people being occupied with the positive side of life, they had little success except in epochs when great terrors were abroad—just before the year 1000, for example, or during famines and epidemics—and, in addition, when people were in a mood to credit Nemesis, because their comfort and good living had gone on too long. Lorenzo says that Thorkild is a victim of acedia, the nightmare of a purposeless existence. And he's in one of the planet's most demanding and responsible posts. You know what a single question from Lancaster Long has done to him. Are you still so eager to tie Azrael into the Bridge System? Against Long's will? When that could do the same to all of Earth?"

Alida put her hands to her eyes. Her head was ringing in confusion.

"You seem to be implying he'd refuse a Bridge! Yet if his people want to proselytise for their beliefs—"

"Supervisor Marquis," Hans said in a level voice, "for a century the Bridge System has constituted the chief reason for people on Earth to carry on about their normal business. What it does is held to justify people's boredom, anger, frustration—their continuing existence, in short. On Azrael they make their lives seem more real by killing and being killed. How better for them to strike at us, who deny what to them is self-evident truth, than by publicly despising what we most prize?"

"But the benefits of having access to the Bridges—"

"Are as nothing to the result of simply saying no."

After a long and fearful silence she said, "I think you must already more than half believe—"

"Don't say that!" he flared. "It's a hypothetical analysis, nothing more! I'm over-extending it as far as I can in the hope that some trifle of counter-evidence will make one of its essential members snap! That's why, if you have no further reason to detain me, I propose to talk with Dr Lorenzo right away, and Responsible van Heemskirk, and Captain Inkoos and anyone else I can get hold of in a hurry! And then, if they can't cure me of my delusion, I shall have to go to Azrael and find the flaw out there. There *must* be a flaw. I *want* there to be a flaw!"

She drew a deep breath. "Yes, of course there must," she said. "As Supervisor of Relations I too have an interest in there being one. Will you meet me this evening to compare notes on what we've been able to find out?"

The proposition was more blatant than any she had made in fifty years, yet she felt the need to reinforce it. She went on, "The higher, the fewer, all right! But not fewer than is unavoidable!"

He thought it over and eventually shrugged. "Very well. I'll call you at nineteen-thirty."

He took his leave. When the door had closed, she said to the air, "In the end you're going to be cruel. But you won't be able to help it. So I have to forgive you in advance. Don't I?"

Then she wiped the silly question from the city-projection and got on with her regular day's work.

IX

---•◆◆•---

Lorenzo's voice emanated from a small white box lying on a carved table. It said, "When people hear the name of Jorgen Thorkild, they think of everything that's associated with it: the Bridge System and the stars it links together, all the marvels that interstellar contact has made possible. But attaining such eminence as yours is not enough. Once attained it must be justified."

"How would you know?" Thorkild said, picking up the box. "You're only a machine."

The air was warm and cloying, syrup-heavy with the scent of the huge flowers covering every bush of the hundreds in the hospital grounds. They were artfully laid out to disguise the supervision and control machinery with monitored the patients wherever they went, whatever they did or said. But for the risk of enhancing the delusions which some of them were suffering from, such as the notion that plants and trees and other objects were talking to them, there would have been no need for identifiable remote speakers like the one Jorgen was now meditatively hefting.

Here and there were shallow pools on whose mirror-still surfaces lay nenuphars, pink, blue and yellow.

He judged the distance to the nearest of them, drew back his arm, and let fly.

"I am a machine, true," the box allowed judiciously. "But the principles upon which I have been programmed, by human beings, remember, are—"

And splash.

Thorkild dusted his hands and sat down. Within minutes what he had done was bound to be reported to Dr Lorenzo, and he or an automatic solido of him would appear to remonstrate. Nonetheless, even that much relief from the machine's tireless arguments would be worth having. Why couldn't Lorenzo get it through his thick pate that what this one out of all his patients wanted most was simply not to have to reason for a while? React, yes; reason—please, no! Not again *yet!* Not when trying to answer a simple question could drive you into a mental blind alley from which there was no escape either to right or left! If he ever found such an escape, it would either have to be upward—into mania—or downward—into suicidal depression. And he didn't want to be confined to any of those choices! He wanted out, sure! But he wanted to find his own way, not one prescribed in advance by never mind how dedicated a therapist. He wanted to find an escape-route as improbable as the path of a Bridge would have been to his own great-grandfather. Right now he didn't know whether it existed. He was clinging precariously to the belief that it wasn't impossible. Which was why he had so far refused to let Lorenzo undertake a total chemical analysis of his body, on the grounds that he was too important (but he hated that term) to risk being destabilised by systemic additives of the kind nowadays routinely prescribed for "transient personality disorder."

Still, there were additives and additives, and the only item now standing on the low table was a refrigerated wineglass. He had no objection to that, or its contents. Possessing himself of it, he sat down on the grass and prepared to contemplate a nearby flowering shrub.

Among whose thick leaves, he suddenly realised, a naked girl was standing, dappled with shadow. She gazed at him, large-eyed, tremulous, like a shy fawn.

"Nefret!" he said. Replacing the glass, he held out his hand.

"I saw you throw the box in the water," the girl said. A hint of awe tingled her voice. "You're lucky!"

"Lucky, Nefret?" Thorkild didn't mind talking to her; he had done so occasionally since they let him out from sedation. But most of the time, he had been assured, one could only talk *to* her, not with her; this was a breakthrough.

She hesitated, looking to left and right among the branches, then chose a thick stem, heavy with gorgeous waxy blossom, which she snapped off near the base. Holding it before her like a torch, seeming to need its luminance before she dared venture on the open lawn, she took a few cautious steps towards Thorkild. He saw she had drawn open eyes on her breasts with mud from one of the ponds.

"Lucky?" Thorkild said again, uncomfortably. She had her own eyes, too, and they were terribly sharp. They reminded him a little of Lancaster Long's.

"They'll cure me," Nefret said. "But not you. You won't let them."

"You can't cure someone who isn't sick," Thorkild offered.

"It's sick to be different," Nefret said. She lowered the raw end of her flowery branch to the ground and began to pick off petals one by one. She didn't look at Thorkild again.

"I'm soft," she said eventually. "I can feel the cure going on inside me now. Like hands shaping wet clay. One day soon I'll be made over entirely. I won't be me any more. This is the third time, so I remember, you see. I'm too soft to fight the changes. All it needs is for me not to notice when they puff my medicine into the air, and there it is, right inside me, like my own breath, and it turns into a new me and I start to behave the way they want, the way they think is right. But you, you're hard. They won't shape you any other way than the way you are. If they go on trying they'll break you into little pieces and dust, and you'll sparkle in sunlight."

"How come you're here for the third time, Nefret?" Thorkild said. She looked far too young; her body was still half a child's, her figure scarcely formed under her brown sleek skin.

"For being different."

"How are you different?"

"Because I don't want to be the same as everybody. I don't want to be made to think I'm happy. If I'm going to be happy I want to *be* happy. Otherwise I'd rather stay the way I am."

A foot crunched on a gravel path, indicating that somebody was arriving in person rather than via solido. She let the branch fall and darted back into the bushes; she had disappeared before the topmost flower touched the ground.

Thorkild took a sip of his wine before turning to confirm that the newcomer was, as he expected, Lorenzo.

"You got here quickly," he said.

"I was on my way already," Lorenzo smiled. A chair stood nearby; hooking it around with one foot, he sat down. "I suppose you threw the therapy-box in the pond?"

"Ah, it must have happened before," Thorkild said with irony. "A shame! That means you probably have it water-proofed."

"Certified proof against anything from liquid air to

liquid iron. So it's another of the things you can't run away from."

"I'm not running away!" Thorkild blasted, knuckles clenching. "I wish I could get you to understand this simple and obvious fact! I am not repeat *not* running away, or hiding, or dodging, or skulking, or ducking out—"

"Then what are you doing?" Lorenzo cut in, with a rasp of authority.

"I'm looking for a place worth running *to!*"

The retort was unexpected; Thorkild had the momentary gratification of seeing Lorenzo at a loss. But it took him only a few seconds, during which he subvocalised a message to his hospital computers and got an answer, to pick a new path forward.

"In that case, Jorgen, why have you not yet found it? You've worked in the Bridge System all your life since completing your education. You've developed such a grasp of it that—"

"That they picked on me as Director at my absurdly early age! So? It wasn't my decision—it was someone else's! Plus the verdict of a bunch of machines!"

"How much older do you think you'd have to be before you were equipped to hold down your job?"

That was a blow below the belt. Thorkild shut his eyes and winced.

"I mean it!" Lorenzo persisted. "Come on!"

"Oh, how the hell can I guess? There were people older than me they could have chosen—there were people younger, come to that!"

"Hmm!" Lorenzo said, and subvocalised a note. Irritated, Thorkild clenched his fists.

"What are you putting on my file now?"

"A comment regarding your attitude towards chronological age. It strikes me as a trifle atavistic."

"And what's that supposed to mean?"

"Are you really interested?"

Thorkild was about to explode, but caught himself. What a neat trap! As soon as he admitted that he was indeed interested in something, there was the risk that he could be treated in the same way as Nefret: moulded like soft clay. He turned his back by rolling over on the grass and contrived to let loose a resounding fart.

"Highly confirmatory," Lorenzo said. "I'll get the computers to work on it right away." He rose to his feet. "Oh, by the way! What I was coming to tell you was that Alida has been inquiring after you. She's called four times in the past two days."

"And you didn't tell me when she was actually on the line?"

"She didn't ask to speak with you. Just how you were."

"Ah, that'll be her conditioned politeness. She's good at it. Well, I've seen enough of that kind of thing to last one lifetime. I'll forget about any attachment I ever had to her and look elsewhere. Do you frown on liaisons between your patients, Doctor? I rather fancy little Nefret. She ran off when she heard you coming. Maybe if you'd go away again she might come back."

"Oddly enough, you mean that," Lorenzo said. He sounded puzzled. Thorkild shot him a suspicious glance. That was the trouble with this man: he was perceptive. Right now the Director of the Bridge System wanted to be surrounded by people who would simply listen without criticising.

"Tell me something," Lorenzo went on. Thorkild cut him short.

"Anything I could tell you, I'm certain you could learn just as easily from my file! Haven't I been monitored and analysed all my life? Would the machines have elevated me to my position of so-called eminence had people not believed that the records they made constituted a tolerable analogue of my personality? Oh, I'm in a state of potential immortality, same as you! In a hundred, maybe in a thousand years' time someone who wants to know what we were like will be able to punch for one particular record out of billions, and there we'll be, eating and drinking and making love and generally going through the human motions, especially as and when we use the Bridges."

"Bridges—human motions," Lorenzo said.

"What?" Beginning to be frightened, Thorkild sat up.

"Sorry, I meant to subvocalise that. I was just entering an equivalence-postulate on the file."

Thorkild scrambled to his feet; he towered over Lorenzo, who remained outwardly calm.

"Oh no you don't! You meant me to hear that!"

"If you can still be angry you haven't lost all contact with the rest of us. You can still be proud!"

"Proud? You must be off your head! I've given up pride."

"When?"

"I know exactly when! The moment I realised all I had to be proud of was how good I am at being used by other people."

"When was that?"

"Haven't I already told you? When I tried to answer Lancaster Long's question, and saw Uskia with a speaker plugged into her navel so her unborn child could eavesdrop on what was happening. And I thought: here I am working like a slave, sweating over everything from petty details to grand policies, standing father to other people's decisions and pretending they're my own, taking the blame if they turn out to be wrong . . . And do I do this for my own sake? No I don't! I do it for superstitious, knuckle-headed, potbellied morons like Uskia! I'm to be proud of *that?*"

"Do you think this is what drove Saxena to kill himself?"

It was the question Thorkild had been bracing himself for. He turned away, muttering, "Should I know? Ask Alida!"

"Haven't you asked her?"

Thorkild grunted and drained his wine-glass.

"You haven't asked her, have you? Because she has refused all forms of intimacy with you, right? And your subconscious has regarded this as defining you inferior to Saxena—"

"For pity's sake, I worked all that kind of superficial nonsense out of my system ages ago! And by myself!"

"That," Lorenzo said judiciously, "I am well prepared to believe. A man who can *be* Director of the Bridge System has no need of minor perquisites like that. He automatically possesses enough other goals to—"

"Goals?" Thorkild yawned hugely. "You could say the same of—of a speck of fungus-spawn shot out by a puffball. It doesn't know where it's going, but it comforts itself with the promise that there's something beyond this patch of leaf-mould. Well, we're past our first patch, and what have we found? More of the same! Result: we're reduced to action for action's sake, growth for the sake of growth."

"And all this was made clear by a few words from Lancaster Long?"

"I guess"—reluctantly—"you could say his question brought it into focus."

"I see." Lorenzo turned this way, then that, pacing back and forth as he continued. "Tell me something else, please—which I can't find on your records, because unspoken thoughts don't appear to the machines you seem to hate so much. Did you ever consider taking time out to raise a family?"

"But parenthood is a full-time commitment! Twenty years minimum!"

"I know, I know! Which is why, all too often, people like you leave it to the common folk, as though twenty per cent of a modern active lifetime were too great a tax on—"

"Shut up!" Thorkild hissed.

Lorenzo almost complied, but reserved the right to enter yet another subvocalised comment on the hospital files. Just before Thorkild's temper betrayed him, he went on, "Very well, you have an effective zero rating as regards parenthood. You're quite unlike Uskia, for example. You—"

"What are you bleating about?"

"It's all a matter of hypotheses"—placatingly.

"You and your hypotheses ought to come up against Lancaster Long, then! If there are more people like him where he comes from, they'll jolt the rest of us when they tie into the System!"

Lorenzo looked suddenly much older. His voice was low and brittle when he said, "They decided not to."

"*What?*"

"Decided not to." Lorenzo forced a wan smile. "You might care to reflect on some of the probable consequences. I already asked my computers to work them out, and as soon as you're willing to show interest in the universe again I'll run them for you. But do you know what the name of Long's planet means?"

Thorkild stood statue-still.

"Azrael is the legendary name of the Angel of Death!" Lorenzo barked. "And it looks as though it wasn't picked at random! If you're so sick of life, why don't you copy Saxena's example instead of taking up my time when I'm sure of a thousand cases worse than yours by tomorrow morning?"

He spun on his heel and stalked away. It was long before the look of shock with which Thorkild watched him go changed to something a little nearer to the human.

X

"But this is wrong," Alida said suddenly. "We aren't being courteous by waiting on him, are we? He's treating us like beggars!"

On comfortable padded chairs in the entrance hall of the house which had been allotted to the Azrael delegation during its stay on Earth, she sat with Moses van Heemskirk and a score of other officials. Laverne should have been among them; he had sent to say he would be delayed, because Uskia planned to return to Ipewell as soon as possible and some minor snags had cropped up in the Bridge contract for her planet.

Many off-world strangers had used this handsome building. Usually the negotiation period had been long enough to allow some stamp of the occupants' personalities—some hint of the character of their home world—to imprint on the place. No trace of Long or his companions could be detected here; there was not even the faint smell of alien cookery which in the past had so often permeated its air. Only now and then someone could be heard issuing a curt order, or crossed the hallway on soft shoes with the swish of a long dark robe.

Moses van Heemskirk gave Alida a bitter smile

which did not seem proper to his round face. He said, "One obstinate man! And we hang on his decision as though on a rope, by the *neck*!"

"Are we wrong?" she wondered emptily.

"How could he be right?" van Heemskirk countered, turning the question deftly and making it somehow far more dangerously valid.

There was a sound of doors opening, and they rose in excitement. People were emerging from the room into which Minister Shrigg had vanished an hour ago.

"Why do we have to rely on him?" someone murmured, barely above a whisper. But all those nearby could hear, and most of them nodded agreement.

Then Shrigg came out, his face set in a stormy glower, flushed to the limits of his bald pate. He scythed through the crowd to the main door and out, dragging his yes-men and attendants in his wake like rubbish whirling in the wake of a fast vehicle. All eyes followed him reflexively. It was not until he was out of sight that Alida—and in the same moment the rest of the watchers—noticed Lancaster Long standing in the open doorway Shrigg had come from.

His face was a mask of cold contempt.

"We were fools to rely on Shrigg!" Alida mourned.

"Could you have done better?" van Heemskirk rasped, and marched towards Long one second before the latter raised his arm to beckon him imperiously. That much of one's pride could still be salvaged.

But to think a single man could hold such power! Merely by calling in question the value of what Earth most prized, he had indeed triggered off the wave of suicides which had been feared. Also there had been riots and other commotion. Anti-Earth parties on a score of other worlds had hailed the news of Azrael's refusal and some of their more hot-headed adherents were openly talking of sabotage.

The heritage of the stars, which humanity had

dreamed of since the cave-days, and here was one man setting it at naught!

Did he realise how much he was going to be hated? Probably. But more than likely he would relish it.

He was saying, "I shall return to Azrael forthwith—I and those who came with me. You will instruct Captain Inkoos to lift her ship off my planet as soon as possible. I've had enough of you and your decadent Earth!"

Unconsciously he rubbed his left forearm with the fingertips of his other hand; Alida realised he was touching the spot where the rattlesnake's fangs had sunk in.

"Oh, we shall certainly do as you say," van Heemskirk declared, defiantly staring up at the beaked face so far above his own. "Until you decide differently. But Earth is old and very patient. There's no hurry."

Alida felt a stir of admiration. His contempt was almost equal to Long's own, but tinged with patronism—as it were: you'll grow up, you'll learn better one day.

Long seemed not to have heard him, though. He said, "I've explained to Minister Shrigg, but he's a wooden-headed booby. I suspect you at least have an inkling of what I'm talking about. I want someone here to recognise the reason why I spurn your gilded bait, why we of Azrael will have no truck with your elaborate toys."

Hans had predicted this, Alida remembered. But it was not good to think of Hans. He too was elusive, the end of a rainbow. She had touched and held him, yet she knew she had never come near him, nor could she ever do so. But his insight was amazing! And the courage which had taken him to the world where Chen had died—where, even now, he was facing the same odds . . . !

"Why waste the time?" van Heemskirk said with superbly affected boredom. "Even machines can diagnose petty jealousy. A child may persuade himself that what adults regard as a tool is nothing more than a toy, to be played around with and, come to that, broken for fear another child may also enjoy it."

"Your gibes don't touch me," Long said. "They come from where you live, in a world remote from reality. It must be for the same reason that what I say cannot touch any of you."

"Must be?" van Heemskirk echoed with irony. "Well, there are degrees of necessity, in my view . . . But hear me out, won't you?"

"I've had enough of your babbling," Long snapped.

"Nonetheless, I advise . . ." van Heemskirk said delicately, and did not end his sentence. But a wave of tension passed among those listening. Alida found herself pressing closer. It seemed as though the fat politician might be going to say something unexpected. Important? *Salvation?*

But how?

"Well?" Long demanded.

Conscious that he had re-established domination, van Heemskirk took his time. He spoke slowly, savouring the words.

"You have made your position perfectly clear by endless repetition. Consequently it will be gratifying for you to learn that immediately you told Minister Shrigg that you absolutely, totally and unqualifiedly abominated the idea of an Azrael Bridge—"

That must be a quotation, Alida realised, for Long bridled: *how could you know my very words?* And van Heemskirk responded by tilting his head, so that light caught on a silvery thread leading from his ear to his vocal cords and then down under his collar: a micro-communicator. Alida wanted to clap her hands. She had not thought of equipping herself with one of those for this crucial meeting, and she was annoyed at her oversight. Meantime the politician was continuing:

"—we took the action you desired. The scoutship *Hunting Dog*, Captain Lucy Inkoos commanding, lifted for space on my authority before Minister Shrigg crossed this hallway. By now she is in tenthousand-kilometre orbit, and will not return to the surface of the planet, though she will remain in the system until further orders."

It was as though the sun came out on a dull day. Smiles exploded on every face except Long's own.

And Alida's. She stood quite frozen.

"But—" Long said after a confused pause, and had to swallow hard. It was a pleasure to see him at a loss.

"But," he went on eventually, "what about me? And my entourage?"

"Oh, what you do is entirely your own affair. We respect the freedom of the individual, here on Earth. But since you are no longer a negotiating team engaged in discussions for a Bridge to your home world, we must require you to vacate this house within twenty-four hours. It is official property and reserved for official guests. Good afternoon."

He cocked one eyebrow impudently at the taller man, turned on his heel, and stomped towards the door. Behind him someone started to chuckle; then it was open laughter, and everyone was joining in. Again, except Long himself, and Alida.

For Hans was on Azrael. Had they allowed him time to leave?

"Return us to your scoutship, then!" Long was shouting. "One of our own ships can rendezvous with her and—"

On the threshold van Heemskirk halted and swung around. "But you abominate the idea of travelling by Bridge," he said in a voice like the edge of a knife.

"And we will not inflict it upon someone who is opposed by reason of conscience. Fend for yourselves, therefore. *Goodbye!*"

"Whose idea do you think it was?" van Heemskirk said bitterly. "I wasn't so clever."

"You mean Hans is still on Azrael!" Alida cried.

For a moment or two van Heemskirk concentrated on the old-fashioned luxury of the car they were riding in; it was a rare experience in the modern world to enjoy the leisurely progress of a private wheeled vehicle, the sight of building-fronts sliding by, the human scale of a mere hundred k.p.h. instead of what in space or even the upper air had for centuries been taken for granted.

At last he gave a nod.

"You left him there!" Alida accused. "Abandoned him!"

"Oh, no. He chose it. He talked about fighting a sort of duel." His voice was uncharacteristically edgy. "That was his actual phrase: him on Azrael, Long here. To the victor the spoils."

"But if he wins, he loses," Alida said.

"I know," van Heemskirk answered with unusual gentleness. "Alida, I do realise that because, as a career politician, I depend on my popularity, my voters, to keep me in office, people like you tend to dump me in the same mental category as Shrigg and others of his stamp. But you've known me a long time now. Is there not a little difference between him and me?"

She forced a nod.

"I'm relieved! You see, I don't mind being what I am, because I think of myself as the sort of person who has to oil the wheels of the social machine. Who more concerned than me when someone throws a bucketful of sand into it . . . ? You've fallen in love with Hans Demetrios, haven't you?"

"Is it so obvious?" she replied dispiritedly.

"It does show a little. And I'm not surprised. I see a faint resemblance to Saxena in him. I hope you don't mind people talking about Saxena now. There was a time, I recall, when you found it unbearable."

"He's dead," Alida sighed.

"Except in your mind, and Jorgen's. It's about time he died there, too. In fact I think in Jorgen's he is now dying. I spoke to Lorenzo yesterday, and he was cautiously optimistic about a breakthrough on that level."

Rubbing his plump hands together as though washing them without water, he added, "I gather it had been some while since you yourself inquired after Jorgen."

At the implied reproach Alida found she was flushing like a teenager. She said, "There'd been no change—no change—no change . . ."

"So you decided you might as well write him off, hmm? It isn't good to dwell on the possibility of failure, whether Lorenzo's or Jorgen's own. Isn't that the long and short of it? And isn't that one of the reasons why, as the centuries pass, fewer and fewer among us—the élite, for want of a better word—dare commit ourselves to parenthood? Making ourselves answerable for a whole other human being, let alone several as they used to, is so fraught with the possibility of failure that we shy away from it. Yet failure, surely, is indispensable. How can success feel three-dimensional without failure to contrast it with?"

"I thought you wanted to talk about Hans!" Alida cut in.

"I do."

She was shaken. What van Heemskirk said reminded her so much of Hans's dry: "I haven't changed the subject."

She said dully, "Very well. Go on."

"Somehow we've become trapped by shame at the risk of failure. We're obsessed by it. In that state you can't face someone whose avowed intention is to make your handiwork seem worthless. More subtly, you can't accept a job that someone else took on before you, and couldn't cope with. Not unless you believe in your heart of hearts that you're better than he was. And that gets harder and harder because every generation since the year dot has selected for the very best among us."

"Are you talking about Jorgen?"

"In a sense. Why did Saxena kill himself, Alida? I never dared ask you before. But if anybody knows, you must."

"I'm surprised you're interested," she said wearily. "But I'm obliged to disappoint you, anyway. He never told me. He never let slip a single hint before he did it."

"Perhaps it would help him to die in your mind if you did work out an explanation. Let me make a suggestion which I personally find useful when I'm more than ordinarily frustrated. Like it or not, there's a tiny handful of people on Earth—come to that, on any inhabited planet—bearing an awesome burden of responsibility. We constitute, we can't avoid constituting, the parent group of the family of humanity. What happens to parents? People look up to them until they in turn become parents. But so few of us actually accept the demands of raising children now . . . All the natural responses which should work themselves out in direct, person-to-person relationships, in our case remain abstract, with infinitely more power to cause psychological damage when things go wrong. Even with you beside him—and I trust you'll take it as a compliment when I say that you're a motherly person, because if you weren't you couldn't have handled your job so well for so long—even with your support, then, Saxena could not face the strain of being a member of the parent group. It wasn't you that let him down, which is what I suspect you feel afraid of. It was the other way around. And, given what has happened to Jorgen, it may simply turn out that the post of Director of the Bridge System is the one role in all of history which no single person can endure. It wouldn't be surprising, would it? Throughout the centuries we've imposed more and more demands on fewer individuals. So—" He concluded with a wave of one plump hand.

She was very pale, but she had been nodding more and more often as he talked. Now she said, "Thank you, Moses. That's a credible insight. I think I shall find it useful. It explains a lot about my attraction to Hans, too."

"As the person brave enough to take over where Chen had failed, yes. In fact I mentioned my theory to him, and he found he was in broad agreement. This was at the meeting when he told me what to do if our best efforts to persuade Long to recant didn't pay off."

"What did he actually say?" Alida put her hands between her knees to stop them trembling.

"That our only hope, if Long proved adamant, was to convince the public that we were right and Azrael was behaving in a petty foolish manner. He warned of a partial failure whatever we did: a wave of suicides, a wave of wilful deaths in risky pastimes. There *is* something damnably attractive about the idea of putting a term to a monotonous existence! That's presumably why people flock to see Rungley, and why Long thought fit to bestow the blessing of publicity on him."

"So he told you to ensure that Long got stranded here."

"Where we can ensure that he is gradually diminished from a mysterious, awe-inspiring stranger to a familiar, rather foolish figure who doesn't know what's good for him or his world."

"You didn't—uh—prompt Hans into staying on Azrael?"

"I may be conceited, but I'd never dream of telling a pantologist what to do! No, he foresaw everything, including a legalistic justification which warrants him doing so under Azrael law."

"He got himself appointed as Shrigg's special investigator into Chen's death?"

"Congratulations, Alida! You're beginning to think like your normal self again. On Azrael they don't have a trial prior to the execution of someone who killed in the course of ritual, but they do have to file a verdict prepared by someone who would correspond, in old-fashioned legal terms, to an examining magistrate. On their own terms they have to put up with him until he's satisfied."

"How about getting him home?"

The plump man hesitated. At length he said gently, "The scoutship will stand by indefinitely, and he can contact Captain Inkoos whenever he likes."

"I see . . . Moses, did you discuss your parent-role theory with Lorenzo? I mean, in connection with Jorgen?"

"I didn't need to. Apparently loss of the direct contact with the future represented by raising children is among the commonest causes of the condition the poor fellow is suffering from."

"The 'black night of the soul'?"

"Precisely."

Alida shuddered. "What a horrible phrase! All by itself it carries one back to the Dark Ages, when people laboured under the burden of crazy superstition—black magic, witchcraft, demons and evil spirits everywhere one turned!"

"That's why Hans is prepared to take his gamble."

"What?" Alida turned in confusion; they were nearing the end of their journey.

"I was instructed not to tell you this until everything had worked out as Hans predicted. But I can do so now. You know the fur hats the men from Azrael wear?"

"Of course!"

"Have you ever seen Long without his?"

"No, I haven't—but what of it?"

"The doctors did, at the hospital where he was taken for his snake-bite. That was how I found out."

"*What?*"

"When his hat is off, you can see on each side of his forehead, just below the hairline, a little puckered excrescence of hardened skin. They said it was almost as hard as a fingernail. In other words, Alida, because he thinks it fitting to his rôle, Lancaster Long is trying to grow horns."

XI

If that one moment in the act of suicide which lies
between the decision and the death could be stretched
to days or weeks, Hans Demetrios thought, it would
best resemble what he was now experiencing. The
hung-on-nothing instant after the chair is kicked
away, before the cord constricts the throat; the seconds between the cliff-top and the rocks; the
intolerable burning of the poison in the gut; the hiss
of air escaping into space, carrying its own sound to
ears that will never hear anything again . . .

Yet there was hope to cling to. He imagined—he
forced himself to believe—that he had located the
weak spot in these people's reasoning. He must chisel
away at it tirelessly until the monolith of their conviction shattered.

Must. For if he didn't . . .

But he refused to let himself think about that.

The people were puzzled at first when the scoutship, giving no warning, lifted from the port, leaving
only the dwarfed figure of Hans standing on the arid
concrete like a lone mourner. He felt at that moment
curiously divided, between regret at what he was los-

ing and eagerness to know whether he was justified in his sacrifice. He compared himself to a starving man who could find no food except a bitter fruit which twisted his mouth even as he choked it down.

It was a little while before a group of silent men came to escort him before one of the local officials known as custodians of propriety. They handled him roughly, but he was prepared for that. In a room walled with brown planks the official demanded the reason for his presence.

Hans answered meekly, hiding his true emotions.

"Your representative, Lancaster Long, refused to permit a Bridge to Azrael, and demanded that we leave your world forthwith. We would not try and force anybody to act against his will. Yet there remains unfinished business. I am here to complete it. I am of rank superior to your own, but shall be content if you address me as an equal."

Since the official was clearly old enough to be Hans's grandfather, he bridled.

"What about Long and his companions?"

Hans gave a measured shrug.

"What they do is of no concern to me. I presume they are still on Earth. Certainly they did not come back by way of the scoutship's Bridge."

That was met with a scowl. "And what do you want?"

"For myself, nothing. For the people of Earth, justice. One of us was killed here."

"The account was regulated. There was an execution. All was done in accordance with the law."

"But it must be shown that your law is just."

"What else is justice but the law?"

"If that is true, why does not every planet have the same law as your own?"

Hans stood meekly blinking, and waited. At length the official uttered barking orders, and guards took him to a cell. Squatting on the hard floor, back into a corner for what support it lent him, Hans reviewed in imagination what must be happening beyond these stark bare walls.

The exact status which entitled Long to speak for Azrael in negotiations with Earth was one of the things that even Jacob Chen had not been able to fathom. Ipewell had been perfectly simple; there was the quasi-religious foundation of the matriarchy, the legend of the Greatest Mother of All whose temporary personification was Uskia—a whole interlocking society to which keys could readily be found. The image of the Grand Lama in ancient Tibet had been particularly indicative. Because there was minimal delegation of authority it had been necessary for Uskia herself to go to Earth; because she was absent, it had been easy to work out how the power-relations between her subordinates operated. The analysis, though complex, was derivable from a few basic assumptions, and though it might need to be modified in the light of experience, once people from Ipewell and other human worlds began to interact, it was fundamentally sound. Hans was sure of that.

But as to Azrael—

It was clear that there was a kind of caste system. If one could compare it with anything, perhaps the structure of ancient Japan might serve as an analogy. More than pedigree, what counted in determining one's caste was a code of behaviour. In the highest caste of all, it could be taken for granted that any member of it would react in precisely the same way as any other to no matter what sort of challenge—up to and including renewed contact with the far-distant mother planet.

In principle, therefore, it would have made no odds whether Long and his entourage had been selected to visit Earth, or a totally different group. It verged on the impossible for someone raised against the background of Earth's society, which cherished individuality, to comprehend such an iron-rigid set of assumptions; yet there was no alternative explanation that fitted half so well.

One had to reach into the far past to gain a glimmer of understanding. Hints and clues abounded—in classical Greece, an artist who had created a master-work would flaw it deliberately, for fear its perfection might excite the jealousy of the gods; also, in many cultures, people had taken their most prized possessions and burned them for a sacrifice. Even to an only child. Even to life itself. And done so as unquestioningly as by reflex.

But who would have dreamed of such attitudes on a planet which had been colonised by a faster-than-light starship, whose culture was as little inclined as Earth's own to imagine capricious supernatural overlords?

Captain Inkoos and the rest of the crew of the *Hunting Dog* knew such concepts as sacrifice and divine jealousy only from their study of history. The fact of existence made its own demands on them, which they were satisfied to fulfil. They regarded their lives as rewarding. They had skills and tactics developed over more than their own lifetimes which had proved to be trustworthy tools. Therefore they had expected nothing out of the ordinary at Azrael, save insofar as every world re-contacted had its own peculiar characteristics. They had even inclined to hope that this planet might be especially remarkable; it was nice, on furlough, to mention what one had recently been doing and find that complete strangers wanted to ask informed questions. Accordingly they had announced their presence, established contact, landed in the place designated, met with officials of the highest caste, offered the Bridge . . .

Nothing had prepared them for the shock which

had so disheartened the scoutship's staff pantologist that he had to resign and make way for Chen . . . by which time the close-mouthed natives had already selected Long and his fellow delegates, and they were on Earth.

Where they still were.

Hans sat in the corner of the chilly cell and willed the rumours to begin. The rigidity of this society implied that everybody must be constantly suspicious of one another's motives. Where the only grounds for trust consisted in the assumption that other people thought identically to oneself, the slightest hint of departure from the common norm must breach that trust. Nobody would yet ask him, Hans, whether Long had chosen to stay on Earth; the very idea he should so have chosen would be unthinkable.

It was his most immediate task to make it thinkable. By adroit implication, he must cause people to worry. Had Long betrayed their code, so he would not dare return home? Despite all his outward scoffing at the decadent ways of Earth, had he let himself be tempted by them? Once posed, such questions would demand an answer. And because they had no channel of communication with Earth—even now, he estimated, they would be discovering the wall of silence he had ordered the scoutship to maintain—their only means of finding out was via himself.

It was a slender thread on which to depend for his life. But he was tolerably certain they would decide to collaborate with him in the hope of learning the truth about Long indirectly. Perhaps they would try to strike a bargain; perhaps they might lose patience and torture him. However it turned out, he would have to rely chiefly on his own resources. He did not even possess one of the computer-belts which Earth's representatives normally wore when travelling off-world; van Heemskirk had offered him his choice of the newest and best, and he had refused, saying, "These people are only human, like myself. It will prove nothing if I can't beat them without machines."

The most he had accepted was a thread-like communicator hidden in his hair. It would enable him to report progress to Captain Inkoos and thus to Earth. But he expected to make little use of it. It did have a second function; it monitored his life-signals, and if they ceased or grew dangerously irregular the *Hunting Dog* would descend snarling from the sky to snatch back, if need be, his still-warm corpse at the cost of anyone who tried to stand in the way. It would be the final proof of the argument he was attempting to defend. A little late for himself, but just possibly soon enough to rescue Azrael.

He concentrated on that one above all his other insights. People like Shrigg, van Heemskirk, Jorgen Thorkild, even Alida who was immensely sensitive to his predicament—they all thought he was taking this gamble for the sake of Earth.

Not so.

He had set out to bring salvation to the planet Azrael.

Days leaked away; he was fed, made more or less comfortable, visited now and then by men who could have been Long's brothers and made polite inquiries concerning his well-being, which he met with muted but unmistakable complaints at not being able to conduct the business he was here for. After a week one of them, whom he had not seen before, glanced around worriedly as though afraid of being overheard—but they were alone and the guard who stood before the cell-door had been sent on some specious errand—and asked whether Long had remained on Earth of his own free will.

Hans concealed his jubilation. He said in a bored-sounding tone what was the perfect truth: "I never met this man Long! I heard he did something which I regard as stupid, and in public. Beyond that . . ."

And a shrug.

"In any case," he added, "Long could have had no part in the death of Chen. He wasn't even on this planet when it happened. I require to speak with those who were and saw it."

Which concluded that particular conversation . . .

Next morning, however, he was at last led from the cell and to a kind of audience-hall, just as devoid of ornament as any other room on Azrael, but sombrely decorated with men in robes of deep rich colours, who stood here and there on the stone-flagged floor like giant chess-pieces. At the centre of the group was a high-backed chair of dark wood, presently vacant.

Stiff from his confinement, much aware of the aroma his clothes must be giving off after so long without washing, Hans preserved his dignity as best he could. He looked with deliberation at each of the men in turn; one returned his gaze with calm appraisal. Very good, Hans thought. That was the one he would direct his attention to, regardless of who came to occupy the chair.

The door creaked open. A stooped old man appeared, helped along by a younger. His robe and hat were as black as space. It dawned on Hans that the garb of the man who had met his gaze was midnight-blue. His own clothing, for no particular reason, was off-white and was now of course marked with dust. Possibly a stroke of luck? At all events it offered an image that one might exploit in argument.

Seated, the old man said in a thin but still forceful voice, "So you're the boy who claims to be senior to our custodians of propriety! You will not do so in my presence. I am Alastair Shang, and I have renounced the right to die in ritual more often than any of my colleagues. I have endured the duty of existence for a century!" He bent aside to utter a wheezing cough. And, recovering, concluded: "It is still open to you to escape the universe at a mere fraction of my age!"

How interesting . . . ! Hans's heart leapt. But he preserved his impassive demeanour.

"I had been informed that medical science on Azrael was atrophying," he murmured. "I will therefore not trouble you with the discrepancy between my apparent and my chronological age. It is entirely irrelevant to the purpose of my stay here. Of which I have already talked at length to several of your colleagues—separately, to my amazement. It had been my impression that the lords of Azrael spoke and acted as one."

"We do!" Shang declared, clutching the arms of his chair and leaning forward with a glare.

"The secretive and confidential visits some of them have paid me in jail do not well match your claim," Hans said, glancing from one to another of the listeners. "However, if you prefer to believe that, I shall not dispute it. I shall only observe that we of Earth act otherwise, and therefore it will be enough for you to justify Chen's death to me alone."

There was a puzzled silence. Shang said at last, "There was talk of an investigation. But one was held here. It was enough. It was under the law he died by. Why do you mount another?"

"It is not another. It is the only investigation. That is, it will be, if you let me complete it. There was no investigation here on Azrael."

"There was!" barked one of the tall men standing near the chair. "I conducted it myself!"

"And you said"—Hans's amazing memory brought

the words to his lips without any need for him to think them out—"it was in the course of ritual, in the view of all, and when one does that, he is deliberate. So you said to Captain Inkoos, did you not?"

"I well recall having done so!"

"But you spoke only of the killer, not the victim. I speak of the victim, deprived of the opportunity to endure the duty of existence for another century or two. Of course, if here on Azrael you have no one whose life is of any value, the significance of what I say will be lost on you."

Beginning to look worried, one of the others bent to whisper in Shang's ear, and after a little thought he did as Hans had been expecting. He signalled to the man in midnight-blue to take up the argument. This latter, smiling with thin lips above a straggly grey beard, stepped forward.

"I am Casimir Yard. You touch on philosophical matters like a child, without understanding. I will attempt to enlighten your ignorance."

"Some would say," Hans countered, "that taking the life of a stranger without consideration for any but one's own selfish desire for oblivion is akin to the action not of a child but a baby, for whom the world beyond its own skin does not exist, save insofar as it can provide immediate gratification, of course. I take it, however, that all of you here present have grown up past that stage, at any rate, or you'd be dead already, wouldn't you?"

One of the onlookers drew a hissing breath, and many fists clenched. Casimir Yard, however, merely sighed.

"Clearly you labour under the delusion that mere existence is worthwhile for its own sake. This is the condition not even of a baby, but of an unintelligent beast, or plant. By the same token, when the individual existence of a mindless organism reaches its term, it is of no account. On the other hand, we who are human—"

Hans cut in sharply. "But you paid not the least heed to the question of Chen's identity! Was the termination of his existence that of a mindless organism?"

Yard replied unperturbed. "We paid him the respect we pay our own: that is, we assumed him capable of a decision to seek oblivion. If this was not his intention, we do not apologise, but regret he was—shall we say?—inferior to ourselves. Looking and sounding human, he must necessarily have been of the lower orders of creation."

"To achieve the goal you set such store by," Hans said, struggling not to grit his teeth at the charge that Chen was an inferior being, "must one not be totally and rationally informed?"

"That is the definition of a superior being," Yard said with confidence.

"Had he not constantly, since his arrival in your midst, questioned you and others like you concerning the motivation of your society and the purpose of your ritual?" Hans stepped back half a pace, sweeping the assembly with his eyes. "I do not address Casimir Yard alone; I address you all, and wish my answer to come from you at random. For you have already declared that all the nobility of Azrael speak and think as one. *You* answer me!" He shot out his arm towards a man standing the other side of Shang's chair.

"It's so," the man admitted reluctantly, not meeting Hans's gaze.

"And you told him—what?"

"That the highest goal of an intelligent being was to be able to choose death, instead of having it occur by accident or the malevolence of an inferior species."

Yard had been tensing visibly; on hearing that impeccably orthodox answer, he relaxed.

"And," Hans pursued, "because suffering is a projection of the ultimate reality of death, it must not only be endured but institutionalised?"

"Why—yes!" the man said, puzzled.

"And because reality is unwelcome, the postponement of death is admirable?"

"Not at all!" Shang shouted, as soon as he had worked out the implication of what Hans was saying. He tried to rise from his seat, but emotion and age combined to betray him, and he subsided into coughing again, waving for Yard to take up the argument he could not advance.

Managing to appear perfectly calm and in total possession of himself, though his heart was hammering and his mouth was bone-dry, Hans said, "Then explain why it is the choice of the nobility of Azrael to endure life as long as possible, if that is not an act of denying reality."

"It is an act of acceptance," Yard said. "And it is given to few to accept for so long."

There were vigorous nods. Hans disregarded them.

"It is therefore incorrect, in your view, to deprive of life someone whose intention is to endure it indefinitely?"

There was a dead silence. Recovering his breath, Shang said, "It is not given to human beings to endure indefinitely!"

"The medical science available on Earth," Hans said, "does at least surpass your own, does it not? Whether this has anything to do with Lancaster Long's continued presence on my home world, I will not venture to guess; I will, though, state as a verifiable fact—and I'm certain that Long's delegation reported this before communication was interrupted—age like Shang's is unremarkable, for anyone may reach it."

"As blindly and purposelessly as a tree!" Shang rasped.

"You attempt to elude my point," Hans countered coldly. "Which is that here on Azrael anyone may be wasted in the course of ritual, regardless of intention."

"That is imprecise," Yard said quickly, before Shang could speak again. "It is always with intention that one takes part in the ritual."

"And the ritual is what lends meaning to existence?"

"Yes!"

"And choosing to take part in a ritual that may end in death is what distinguishes the mindless from the intelligent orders of creation?"

A pause. But, reluctantly: "Yes!"

"And killing a stranger entitles one to be killed, which is access to the sole reality?"

"Well—yes!"

"And it is as a symbol of your dedication to what in the mythology of ancient Earth would have been called the powers of evil that you put horns on your foreheads?"

Before the implications of that had sunk in, Hans had closed the gap between himself and Shang with three long strides, and sent the old man's hat flying with a wild sweep of his arm. Under it, his pate was almost bald. But on the waxy skin revealed where his hairline must once have been, there were indeed two deformed lumps, each as large as the top joint of Hans's thumbs, around which smeared a reddish area of inflammation. Shang cried out feebly and those about him rushed to retrieve the hat—not to restrain Hans, who was able to return to where he had been standing and confront them all.

"I understand now," he said in his loudest and clearest voice. "I understand what you never dared explain to Chen!"

Yard seemed about to say something; even he, though, held back, folding his bony fingers into his palms. They all waited like criminals in the dock attending the verdict of a jury of one man ...

How in all of space could voluntary disfiguration have attained magical status in a society that still possessed at least interplanetary spacecraft? How could membership of an élite that should have been an intelligentsia be reduced to mere willingness to endure a trivial cicatrisation? It was like branding meat-animals—!

Oh, no. Wait a second. It wasn't. It was far more like—

But Hans had no more time to work out the details, sprung to his mind in a flash which Jacob Chen should have enjoyed. Would have, except that the underlying impulse was now so nearly forgotten, back on Earth and on all other inhabited worlds—

No time, no time! He must deliver himself of the ultimate challenge to which he believed they would have no answer, on which he had staked his own life and the future of the planet.

He said, "You have insisted over and over that your wish is for death. You have insisted that it is right and just and proper that whoever kills in the course of ritual shall himself be killed.

"But what you have overlooked is that if you persuade us of the truth of what you say ..."

He paused for maximum effect, and saw they were licking their lips, swallowing hard, shifting from foot to foot as they sought a way out of the trap they had created for themselves. Shang had apparently fainted, but none of them was paying him any more attention.

"What you have overlooked," Hans resumed, "is

that we too can kill. By any of a hundred methods, we can kill you."

And there it was, exposed in all its nakedness: the same dilemma which had impaled Chen, translated into terms that spiked an entire planet.

Are we wrong? Then we have lived a lie, and our existence is pointless, our attempts to bring reality into our lives by confronting ourselves with pain and death are trivial nonsense.

Are we right? Then we have given those out there, more powerful than ourselves, the justification to put an end to us as some of us have put an end to one of them.

In that terrifying moment before any of the spokesmen for Azrael found a way to respond, Hans recognised that their predicament was his: the need always to be absolutely right. And became the first pantologist to admire the strength which might flow from being wrong.

Later, he found comparisons from the far past to explain and justify his reaction. To the end of his days, his favourite was the image of an officer assigned to punish conscientious objectors during one of Earth's last wars, who sent back his medals and preferred to shake their hands rather than his general's, because they had chosen to undergo worse torment than anyone who agreed to shoot at unknown so-called enemies.

But the torment had been unnecessary and fruitless. And he already knew that much when he forestalled what Yard was struggling to utter, and rubbed in his crucial point.

"As I told you, I'm here to report on the murder of Jacob Chen. I shall proceed to do so. Were you to hinder me, it would be possible for the ship which is still in orbit to signal others. Hundreds of others. It would be possible for such ships to make your planet a desert, and thereby fulfil your desire. You need only speak the word."

With a certain grim humour, he appended, "As a matter of fact, the *Hunting Dog* alone could do the job. But it would take rather a long time."

XII

Insofar as he was capable of formulating any intention during the period that followed Azrael's refusal of a Bridge, Thorkild had had it in mind to escape into daydreams among the flowering bushes and the lily-ponds, until someone brought the blessed news that the Bridge System could not function with a director *in absentia*, so another person had been appointed to take over. After that . . . well, he would see.

And indeed he managed his ambition for some while. Now, however, there was a hammering echo in his mind, striking responses he could not shut out. *Damn* Lorenzo for telling him news he would have died rather than learn! It must have been with malice aforethought; Lorenzo did nothing without calculation.

He steadfastly refused to watch or listen to newsreports. That didn't save him from knowledge of the most probable consequences. Imagination conjured them up in all-too-convincing form, and they kept getting between him and the tapes he viewed, the books he read, the music he tried to lose himself in. He had been reminded irrevocably of the outer world, and his defences were now breached beyond repair.

He was not certain whether Lorenzo had realised, or was still merely hoping for such an outcome; so far as possible, he was preserving his pose of total indifference. But though it had for a while been genuine, a pose was what it had become. He could no longer avoid feeling guilty about the inevitable suicides and other needless deaths which must be following on from this insult to all Earth chiefly cherished. He cursed the fact that he had been born with a conscience, and could not evade it. Seeking distraction, he called on all the computerised resources the hospital could put at his disposal. He tried playing games, from chess to go, from poker to nith-and-rel, only to discover that the machines had been ordered to operate at maximum analytical levels. Angry, he found he was envying the other patients whose bruised personalities were being cosseted by allowing them at least the illusion of beating the machines. Of course, he said nothing to Lorenzo, for he knew only too well what sort of sarcastic answer he would get.

Exhausting himself in violent physical activity was also useless; it was as though his body knew better than his mind when it was tuned to a healthy pitch, and after about as much exercise as he had been accustomed to all his adult life he could no longer lose himself in what he was doing. Instead, he began to be able to think about what he wanted most to shut away from consciousness.

Then, one day, he woke to find a tune echoing through his head. After some struggle, he identified it as the melody of the song Koriot Angoss had been singing the morning of their discussion about Rungley. He welcomed the fact that it would not leave him, and later in the day called for an electric keyboard, which he carried out into the garden. As a boy he had shown some musical aptitude, and had not wholly lost it. A few hours of clumsy fumbling, and he found he could reproduce the tune complete with proper harmonies.

Thereafter he occupied himself chiefly in sitting by his favourite pond, playing from memory or improvising. Sometimes other patients came and listened, sitting around him on the grass, but he never answered when they tried to talk to him.

Today, however, he had been completely alone, and he had played so long his fingers were growing stiff. He let them lapse into a sort of slow lament, feeling after each note without conscious direction.

Suddenly he hit a raucous polychord and slammed shut the lid of the keyboard. It was no use any more! He could not escape the knowledge in his mind. Long had spurned the offer of a Bridge. An act so completely without precedent implied an underlying purpose. It was his own sense of purpose that Long had stolen. He needed to know why.

He would have to go back.

As the decision crystallised, he looked up. At first he did not recognise the girl facing him, for she was clothed, and he had never seen her that way before. Then he realised.

"Nefret?" he said.

She stood with hands folded demurely in front of her. Her long dark hair was gathered on her nape. Her face was calm. But out of her eyes looked something pathetic, like the spirit of a caged wild beast.

She made no immediate answer, and he went on, "Are you leaving? Are you cured?"

"Yes, they cured me," she said. She folded abruptly at the knees, looked up at him from below. "That is, I am to be allowed to go away today."

"Well—ah . . ." The words sounded hollow, but he uttered them anyway. "Well, I wish you the best of luck. And—and do you know something?" This emerged with a hint of audible surprise.

"What?"

"I shall miss you. I've grown really very fond of you."

"I wish you hadn't," she said with a trace of bitterness, her dark eyes roaming anywhere but his face.

"Why?"

"Because of the reason I decided to let them cure me."

The statement was full of terrible overtones. He leaned forward, pushing the keyboard aside.

"Which is—?"

"I want to kill myself, and here they won't let me."

He stared in horror. For an instant her face became Saxena's, not as in the smiling portrait which adorned the Director's office, but as he must have looked in death, distorted by the poison which had given him release. Then, as so often in nightmare, the Saxena-face became his own.

The illusion passed, leaving him shivering although the air was warm. He said, "Aren't you afraid that if they hear you say that they'll—?"

She cut in impatiently. "Oh, they're not eavesdropping on me any more, not since this morning when my discharge was approved and I stopped being officially a patient. Nor on you, by the way. Did you not know?"

In fact, Thorkild had begun to suspect so; it had been days since any attempt had been made to keep him within earshot of a therapy-box. But that had its reverse side: it could imply (and he suspected Lorenzo meant him to reach this conclusion) that without his being aware of it his treatment had been completed and it only remained for him to realise the fact. Which, in actuality, had just this very moment happened—

But he had no wish to accept that he had been brilliantly out-manoeuvred in his attempt to remain certifiably insane. Mainly to prevent himself thinking about it, he said, "But why, Nefret? With a whole lifetime before you!"

"Because it's the only way to stop the world." She plucked at the hem of her unaccustomed shirt, which she wore awkwardly, like a splint. "Do you remember how I once said to you that I thought I was soft, like clay, and you were hard, like glass, and they would break you before they changed you? I've been watching you, listening to your music. And I know now that I was wrong."

"How do you mean?"

"You're being gnawed at from within. You fidget without reason. You lapse suddenly into silence and stare at nothing. One day soon you're going to give in, and you'll go back to where you came from, and you won't be able to remember why you left. I thought you were hard. No one is hard. So I've let them shape me the way they want, and when I die it won't be me I've killed, but this stranger."

She made an unhappy gesture up and down her body, touching her clothes here and there as though the very feel of them disgusted her.

Thorkild shivered anew. He said, "Nefret, why did you turn out different? What led them to send you here?"

"Oh . . . ! Because of what I wanted. Because I didn't want what I was offered."

"What did you want, then?"

She gave him a curious look. "You know, it's strange!" she exclaimed. "I have the feeling that I know you so well, and yet I know nothing about you except your name and the job you used to hold, and you know even less about me. It's all very simple. I'm uncontracted. My father was on the Earthside staff from Glory, and my mother refused to join him when he went home. The contract was dissolved and my legal guardian is a man in a government office."

"Still?"

"I'm not even seventeen yet. I have another year to go before I'm independent."

"And it was he who had you sent here—didn't you say twice before?"

"Oh, it's not a question of a *he!*" She pulled a face. "It's a *they*. I could fight one person. But the huge imponderable shadowy force behind a bureaucrat—you can't overcome that. I tried. The first time I ran off with a spaceman to Indonesia. I knew it was futile to try and escape that way, but it was kind of fun. I tried to explain, but they'd made up their minds beforehand that I must be crazy and they sent me here. And then I tried to kill myself and failed. And the latest time I think I *was* crazy. I tried to get away by Bridge."

Thorkild clenched his fists. "Was that by any chance the day Director Saxena died?"

"That's right. That's why I tried it then. I thought there might be enough confusion for me to slip through. But I didn't allow for the fact that machines don't have emotions. The computers caught me and I was sent back here."

Thorkild was silent for a long time, thinking over the case as he had seen it from the impersonal heights of top administrative level. It had been the first decision he had been called on to make after taking over. It had looked so simple, so routine . . . He remembered gazing down from the vantage platform before van Heemskirk arrived with Long and Uskia, and wondering what became of human importance so far below. Well, now he had at least part of an answer. But what use it might be, he couldn't tell.

Having waited for him to say something else, Nefret spoke again.

"At least there's a world for people like me now," she muttered. "If I can't escape during the next year, then I know I can once I'm of age. I can go to Azrael and do what Jacob Chen did. Only the difference will be that that is what I really want."

"But it can't be!" Thorkild burst out.

"Why not?" She fixed him with her burning dark eyes. "Why shouldn't I be allowed to want what a whole planetful of other people turns out to want?"

She must have kept in touch with the news about Azrael, which Thorkild had deliberately ignored. His mind raced.

"Because—well, because when you tried to get away by Bridge we hadn't discovered Azrael! Anyhow, they refused to have a Bridge there, didn't they?"

"Oh, I guess they'll change their minds. Earth will work them over, same as Dr Lorenzo has worked over you and me. Even if it takes more than a year, some of Azrael is here already. There's an Azrael Society now—didn't you know? They're establishing temples to hold ceremonies like the one Jacob Chen was killed at. Lancaster Long has been made their honorary president."

A thrill of terror trembled down Thorkild's spine. What was Rungley's snake-handling compared to this subtle and disastrous psychological infection? Yet in what Rungley did it was almost as though he had foreseen Long's influence bodied forth . . .

"You're evading my point," he persisted. "Where were you going when you tried to take a Bridge? To Glory?"

"No, I wasn't setting off to find my father," she said wearily. "That's what they all kept trying to tell me, because it was a tidy capsule explanation. But what's he to me? A biological accident! I wouldn't know him if he met me in the street!"

Abruptly Thorkild grew impatient. He said, "You've told me a lot about what you don't want. Tell me something you could want—something that might make you choose to live."

The girl looked at him with puzzled eyes. She hesitated a long while. Finally she said in an altered voice, "I guess . . ."

"Go on!"

"I guess if I could want anything more, it would have to be . . . anything that matters."

"That's it," Thorkild said. "That's the only thing that anyone can want."

Abruptly a solido manifested three metres away. It was Lorenzo. Viewing them through one of the countless hidden cameras that beset the garden, he nodded to Thorkild but addressed himself to Nefret.

"They're waiting for you at the entrance," he said. "You can go now."

Obediently, like a well-trained dog, Nefret stood up. As she made to turn away, however, Thorkild gestured for her to wait. He rose to confront the image of Lorenzo.

"I don't seem to have seen you much these past few days," he said.

"Why should you?" Lorenzo answered cuttingly. "I've been busy! In case you haven't noticed, there's been an epidemic of transient psychoses like your own. Tens of thousands of people have had the foundations of their existence undermined, and most of them don't have the advantages which led you to help yourself."

"Are you classifying membership in the Azrael Society as *a priori* evidence of mental derangement?"

"Ah, I take it Nefret told you about that. I'm obliged to her. I meant to do so myself, but I've been too rushed. How do you feel, now the subject's come up, about the fact that the stranger who kicked your mental feet from under you is enjoying the sort of planetary adulation you didn't get as Director of the Bridge System?"

For an instant Thorkild was so angry he could have struck out at the doctor—would have, but for remembering that this was only a solido image. Breathing hard, he said, "I think his followers must be a lot crazier than I am. You've beaten me. I'm going back."

Lorenzo's face exploded into a grin. "Well, *well!* I've been hoping to hear you say that, but I wasn't really expecting it for another week or more! You presumably realised, though, that I'd re-categorised you, and it was only a matter of time?"

"Oh, score your points off me!" Thorkild rasped. "It's what keeps you going. I still haven't figured out all of what keeps me going, but I do know one thing for certain."

"Which is—?"

"I hate Lancaster Long for despising what I've dedicated my life to!"

"That makes every possible kind of sense. Have dinner with me this evening and talk it through, and tomorrow—"

"No. Now. You just told Nefret that 'they' are waiting to take her away. Who are 'they'?"

Lorenzo betrayed a hint of irritation. "I guess somebody sent by her legal guardian."

"Tell 'them' to go away," Thorkild said. "I just made an interesting discovery. I'm one of 'them'—and I'm thoroughly ashamed of it!"

As though against his will, Lorenzo began to nod. "Go on," he invited. "So far I don't quite see—"

"Although very likely your machines did," Thorkild cut in. "Well, never mind. But it can't have been sheer chance that led to Nefret winding up in my company so often, hm? And I don't believe you gave orders for it, did you?"

"As a matter of fact, no." Lorenzo looked slightly discomforted. "Of course, once you'd begun to show such interest in her, and she in you, I did authorise—"

"Stop trying to claim more credit than is due you! But don't worry; that's a side-issue. What's central is this. 'They' committed Nefret in your care, didn't they? She was trying to get off Earth by Bridge the day Saxena killed himself. I was his replacement. I stamped the official seal on an order for her committal. I didn't take the slightest personal interest in the case. I'd already gone too far towards dehumanisation. As I recall the law in this respect, though, since she was under Bridge City jurisdiction, her guardian was acting as an agent for the Bridge authorities—for me, in other words. Better check with your computers, but I'm ninety-nine per cent certain that you'll find Nefret is my legal ward."

Lorenzo was staring from one to other of them by the mediation of the camera.

"And you want that?" he demanded.

"Yes, very much. How about you, Nefret?"

She hesitated. At last she said in a whisper, "I think I'd like it to be true. Is it?"

"Just a moment!"

Lorenzo vanished, but for so brief an instant neither of them had had a chance to say anything before he reappeared. He was beaming again.

"Correct!" he announced.

"Good!" Thorkild said briskly. "You haven't officially discharged her yet, have you?"

"No. I simply have to make her over into the care of a 'fit person', as the jargon goes."

"Then I'm your fit person. I'm going to try and provide Nefret with what she wants—simple enough, you'd imagine, because all she wants is anything that matters, but even though I personally want exactly the same I can't have found it yet, not if Long could dishearten me so completely. Nonetheless, perhaps we can help one another find it."

He held out his hand to Nefret. She clasped it in both of hers and drew close.

"Speaking of Long," Lorenzo said after a pause, "apart from hating him, how else do you feel about the guy?"

Thorkild stared for a moment. Then, unexpectedly, he laughed.

"Grateful! That probably sounds like a paradox, but if he hadn't insulted me—he and his whole damned planet—by calling the work I've devoted my life to a piece of empty foolishness, I might have gone right on suspecting that it might be until I was past hope or help. But that's not so. I can't think of any way to prove it, short of beating him over the head, but I'm going to. I swear it!"

"I remember suggesting that so long as you could still be angry you weren't a forlorn case," Lorenzo said. "You've found a cause. Hang on to it. People need causes above all."

Nefret had disregarded most of the last exchange; she was wrapped up in herself. Now she burst out, "Is it true or am I dreaming? Is it really true that somebody I actually know is going to be my guardian, instead of that—that *bureaucrat* who's haunted me so long?"

"That's the idea," Thorkild said, nodding. "Like it?"

She bit her lip to restrain a sob, but her eyes filled and overflowed, and she clutched his hand so hard it hurt.

"A very satisfactory outcome," Lorenzo pronounced. "Though I don't know what the man will say who's been waiting so long to collect Nefret."

An automated helicopter was assigned to rush Thorkild and Nefret back to the Bridge Centre. The news had spread already, and fervent congratulations on his recovery rang out from its communicator almost before they were under way. He was as polite in answering as he could be while comforting his companion; she was weeping openly now, and whispering over and over, "I never thought it would come right! I never dared to!"

His arm around her, his hand mechanically stroking her hair, he sought to concentrate on the problem which now confronted him. Somehow he must persuade the people of the planet Azrael that their view of the universe was wrong—that the subjective purpose human beings found in their lives was no less real than the objective events inflicted by blind nature, such as pain and death. Indeed, he began to argue to himself, one might well claim they were *more* real, insofar as reality could only be defined by reference to perception.

He set his jaw grimly. He was going to get Azrael tied into the Bridge System. Somehow. Some day. And be damned to Lancaster Long!

But, as the helicopter descended towards the roof of the Bridge Centre, his eye was caught by a crowd of people on the ground. They were all clad, as he could see even at this distance, in copies of Long's own garb, the dark robe and the tall hat. At least they were to begin with. As he watched, some of them began to rip off their clothes, fling them down, and stamp and spit and even urinate on them.

Thorkild stared in disbelief. Then it occurred to him to punch the helicopter's communicator for a news broadcast; everywhere on Earth there were a score of them available at any hour of day or night.

If that was the Azrael Society, as he suspected—

Then all else was driven from his mind as the screen of the communicator lit with a single huge and glowing headline:

AZRAEL ACCEPTS BRIDGE!

XIII

Patient though he was, Hans at times came close to despair. He had been correct in his assumption that Casimir Yard was the opponent who mattered, more than Shang or any other of the select clique of custodians who had arrayed themselves against him. Little by little, thanks to this confrontation which Chen had never achieved, he was able to analyse the true structure of Azrael's culture in a way which even its own members were ignorant of. All of them accepted that the principles underlying their behaviour were not only correct, but indispensable to the proper ordering of society. The notion that people could live under other types of government was so remote they could scarcely reason about the possible forms such governments might take, and it was useless to explain to them how their pain-cult had evolved solely because it was adapted to this dismal, hostile planet where life was an endless round of boring struggle for the means of survival, but not to any more welcoming and tolerant world. As far as they were concerned, it offered an infallible means for even the lowliest citizen to make his existence significant by commission of an act no animal could conceive. The emphasis was on the lowly aspect. The élite were those who opted to go on teaching their doctrines without yielding to the temptation of killing.

There was logic behind this attitude, but it was logic of so nightmarish a form that even Hans, who had begun where Chen had left off, was sometimes terrified to reason out its necessary consequences. Population limitation was involved; so was something akin to the palace coups of Byzantine Earth; so too was the emotion known in late pre-atomic culture as *Weltschmerz*, suffering due to the world's inadequacies. Yet, paradoxically, those who felt this agony most keenly were also those who clung most tenaciously to life . . .

It was no paradox to them, naturally.

All this Hans learned, and more, in the course of the inquiries he was reluctantly permitted to conduct, mainly at Yard's insistence, on the grounds that no matter how perfectly propriety had been preserved on Azrael, Hans and those who had sent him were ignorant barbarians who needed to have everything spelled out to them, like children. No records were kept of those who attended such rituals as the one that cost Chen his life; however, the participants remembered because they were rare and climactic events for any given individual, and he was enabled to meet and talk with them. A horrifying picture grew in his mind, of dirt and squalor and starvation, building towards such a fury of frustration that murder and execution ultimately seemed like a desirable release. Never, though, was this impulse directed toward those who had created and now maintained this miserable society. It was invariably directed against one's fellow sufferers.

One might have said: "Small wonder, then, that the nobility are afraid of introducing the Bridge! Everyone will want to emigrate!"

But that was over-facile. This planet was its people's home; most likely, were a Bridge available, ninety per cent of them would be afraid to risk travelling by it, and of the other ten, half at least would come home thankfully, victims of culture-shock.

Trapped, in other words, by their own ignorance and deprivation.

This was why Hans had set out to bring what he regarded as salvation to Azrael. It seemed to him incredibly unjust that human beings, as intelligent no doubt in at least some cases as himself, should be locked into this cycle of poverty when the planet's resources were adequate to set them free. He had been appalled by the primitive living-conditions enforced on the mass of the population, when knowledge to transcend them had been freely available when the colony was established.

Nobody would talk about its origins, but he had investigated, and was fairly sure Azrael had been settled by a dissident group of so-called libertarians, whose dream had soured under the impact of alien climate, alien disease, and alien predators, so that their attitudes reversed abruptly, and they abandoned their belief in the perfection of the individual in favour of a naïve distortion of the "survival of the fittest".

Now there was no room for pleasure, and that offended him. Be it only the refined delight he himself found in conquering an intractable problem, Hans Demetrios held that people should be entitled to enjoyment. It was the right reward for existence. Oblivion could come later.

Little by little, he hinted at this idea to those who accompanied him on his investigative rounds. They dismissed what he said with incredulity, or at best with a harsh laugh—the only laughter he had heard since his arrival.

Alone among them all, Yard rebutted Hans's arguments with arguments of his own. He was the grand master of this planet's weird casuistry . . . chiefly, Hans thought, because he believed in it the least, could stand outside it and take a more nearly objective view than his colleagues. At any rate, he was the only one who seemed capable of hypothesising an alternative way of life and drawing accurate conclusions concerning it.

On the last day to which his inquiry could be protracted, the day after the last person involved in the ceremony when Chen was killed had testified that all were voluntarily present, all took the risk willingly one with another, all might have done what the killer did, all might equally have been his victim, by pure chance, Hans was reduced to despair. For that was also the day when Yard informed him with confidence that—assuming Hans himself to be as exact a representative of Earthside culture as Yard of Azrael's —Earth would never do as had been threatened. Lacking the insight of those who colonised Azrael, he said, they could never regard one man's death as reason to depopulate a planet. Only those who had attained contempt for life could make such a decision. Had the positions been reversed, it would have been a different matter.

"You mean," Hans suggested, "that if Long had died of his snake-bite, you would have accepted the Bridge because lacking other contact with Earth you could otherwise not have exacted revenge?"

It was a brave attempt; it failed. Yard brushed aside all recollection of Long.

"He betrayed us!" he rasped. "You trapped him. A rational person would have foreseen the risk of having his retreat cut off. He was insufficiently alert. Yet it was as well that we selected him. Almost any other of us would have been a greater loss."

That added one more factor to Hans's social analysis, and effectively completed it. But before he could do what he felt now was imperative—signal the *Hunting Dog* to come and fetch him, because the rest of what had to be done constituted a long-term project—Yard had signalled to two men who all today had been following him like a bodyguard.

"Return him to his cell," he instructed. "He will remain there until Long and his delegation are sent back from Earth. And on the way shave his head. We've detected signals emanating from him when he's alone, and I suspect there's something hidden in his hair."

The cell-door closed on the ruin of Hans's hopes. He had been so confident when he realised these people needed to brand themselves as a prop for their convictions; he had thought they would prove vulnerable to the horns of the dilemma he had created . . . and instead they had mercilessly exposed the flaw in his own position, or at any rate one of them had. Now, instead of bringing them salvation, he was condemned to stay here until the cessation of signals from his communicator obliged Captain Inkoos to order her ship back from orbit and retrieve his corpse. Detachment of the device from his scalp would register on the ship's detectors as though he had been killed. Very shortly he might be. And because he had been beaten, he felt it didn't matter if he was.

Unable to sleep at night, unable to concentrate on her work by day, Alida Marquis could think of nothing but the predicament Hans had voluntarily wished on himself. Over and over she reviewed the data Chen had filed before he died; over and over she played the tapes of what Long had done and said since his arrival on Earth. There was a great deal of the latter now, and the existence of an Azrael Society was multiplying problems almost by the hour. Uskia was known to be offended by the way the Supervisor of Relations was neglecting her, but that was a minor nuisance. Work was proceeding on the creation of an Ipewell section in the Bridge City, and most of the rest of the work could be left to the machines. Ipewell was, although unique, well within the parameters established by contact with other human worlds.

Azrael was utterly different.

Why—why—*why* did Hans rely so much on those artificial horns? Surely they implied a capacity for self-delusion! Externalising one's beliefs to a symbol like that was a mark of society after primitive society which had collapsed under its own misconceptions. Circumcision—cicatrisation—tat-tooing—clitoral excision—all sorts of mutilation had been exploited to brand people as members of an exclusive group, keep them isolated and identifiable among the hordes of infidels, goyim, pagans, or whatever . . . And the outcome was what? The interstellar society created by the Bridges, whose members met—at least in the persons of their Earthside representatives—in the giant city she could see spread out below the windows of her office. Pacing back and forth, gnawing her lip, she stared achingly at that marvellous panorama, or sometimes at its miniaturised version in the transparent depths of her table, as though by mere inspection she could unravel the mystery.

Hans had overlooked something. She grew more and more certain of it. And he had staked his existence—worse, his sanity—on his assumptions. She had actually believed that he was going to work a miracle; he had seemed so confident . . .

The solido projector uttered its priority override signal and all of a sudden she found herself about to walk through the portly figure of van Heemskirk. She stopped dead.

The politician was mopping his forehead with a kerchief that matched his yellow robe. He said without preamble, "I thought you'd better hear this before I tell even Shrigg. Captain Inkoos reports that all signals from Hans's communicator have ceased. Either it's failed, which is unlikely, or it's been ripped off his head, or he's dead. She needs authority to proceed and wants to know on which assumption."

Alida's hands curved into claws; her nails pressed painfully into her palms.

"If he did beat them, as he promised," van Heemskirk pursued ruthlessly, "they could very well have killed him for his pains. Couldn't they?"

She stood there swaying, eyes closed, in the grip of a lightning-flash of insight, as though it had taken the belief that Hans too could be killed to bring all her thoughts into focus. But it was her job, and she had gradually become extremely good at it.

"Alida!" van Heemskirk said in alarm. "Are you listening to me? Are you all right?"

She opened her eyes. With painfully correct articulation she said, "Don't tell Shrigg. Not yet. Don't answer Captain Inkoos. Let me put some questions to some people and I'll call you back."

"What?" The plump man blinked rapidly. "What questions? What people?"

"Maybe not so much the people as their machines," Alida muttered. "But Laverne is one, and Lorenzo is the other. Hold for five minutes. As you love me and Hans, Moses, hold for five more minutes. *I think I got what Hans has overlooked!*"

And, she glossed privately, even if I haven't, then this instant when I can make myself believe I know more than a top pantologist is still going to remain a treasured memory ...

In fact it was less than the promised five minutes before she called van Heemskirk back, very pale, speaking in a voice barely louder than a whisper.

"Moses, Laverne thinks I must be right and Lorenzo

is sure of it. What we have to do is this! Listen carefully!"

A while ago a peal of thunder had rolled across the dismal city, and made the walls of Hans's cell shiver. Well, that was nothing new or remarkable. Folded up like an unborn child, he was lost in a miasma of self-pity at his own incompetence.

Suddenly the bolts of the door were drawn aside, screeching. He recovered enough of his self-possession to rise and greet the new arrivals standing. But they were only a pair of guards, who chivvied and jostled him back to the hall where he had formerly confronted Shang and his colleagues.

This time the high-backed chair was occupied by Casimir Yard, and his expression was that of a man who has tasted wormwood.

He said without preamble, "It seems we must consent to your crude blackmail, and accept the imposition of a Bridge."

Hans almost fainted; with all his might he clung to consciousness. As though this was precisely what he had been expecting all along, he said, "Very well, I'm glad for your sakes that you finally saw sense. You understand the conditions attached—that anyone of legal age may travel by it once it's been installed?"

Yard muttered something inaudible, making a gesture as to brush aside a fly. And continued, "You will be taken to the spaceport at once. The ship will descend to fetch you. And I hope very much that I shall never set eyes on you again."

He rose and stormed away.

After that things happened to Hans in such a rush he scarcely had time to register them. Suddenly, it seemed, he was standing on the spaceport in a grey drizzle, and the ramp of the *Hunting Dog* was being lowered, and there were two women advancing to meet him. Captain Inkoos he had naturally expected, but the other was Alida Marquis.

Taken aback, he knew he had to say something. All that offered itself was the damning admission, "I—I was wrong, Alida!"

A look of horror crossed her face as she made to embrace him. Taking a step back, she demanded, "They refused the Bridge—again?"

"No—no!" Bewildered, Hans shook his head. "It's just that I don't understand why they did accept it! It wasn't because I reasoned better than they did!"

"Ah, but you did!" She seized his hand and gazed into his eyes. "You reasoned so well that you made it clear why they must—to *me*, if not to *them!*"

He stood transfixed for long seconds. Then the implication of what she had said began to sink in. From a dry throat he said, "Spell it out."

"But it was all implicit in what you said about Lancaster Long! You said he could let himself be bitten because he didn't know he would be killed. If he'd wanted to die, deep down in his guts, he would have killed somebody. That's the pattern he was raised to. But he let the snake bite him because he'd seen Rungley bitten and knew that at least some people recovered. So long as there's a chance of survival, he and his kind will gamble on it. He didn't refuse therapy when they took him to the hospital, did he?"

"It's coming clearer," Hans said, eyes focused on another world. "Go on!"

"The same pattern holds with the élite that wear the devil's horns! Every time they decline to take part in the ritual that may lead to them being killed at random, they have to pay, and that involves irritating the area where horns are made to grow!"

"You found this out from back on Earth?"

"No, not *found* it out—*worked* it out! It occurred to me to ask Laverne and Lorenzo what they would deduce if a patient from a foreign planet presented at an earthside mental hospital with all of Lancaster Long's symptoms!"

Thunderstruck, Hans gaped and threw his hands in the air. "Obvious!" he said as soon as he could. "And it never occurred to me! So simple a question!"

"What was it?" Captain Inkoos demanded, glancing from one to the other of them.

"Why!" Hans exclaimed. "*Are they actually insane?*"

She rounded her mouth and whistled. "You know, I'd never thought of that! I'm too used to people being—well, less than crazy. Capable at least of organising their lives."

"And so are the people of Azrael," Hans said, frowning now as the full extent of the consequences gripped him. "But it's almost a non-human response, and . . . Never mind, I'll work the rest out later. What I want to know right now is this. How the hell did you bust through their armour against reality?"

"Oh, you must have heard it going off, surely!" Alida said, and glanced at the captain. Who shrugged.

"Well, I guess it was well within auditory range. Mark you, I never expected to be called on to issue such an order, and I sincerely hope that any inquiry will exonerate me from—"

"What did you do?" Hans rasped, advancing on her.

"Shot a multimegaton torpedo into their northern ocean about five hundred kilometres from here and sent an artificial tsunami over a string of coastal villages. I hope nobody was seriously hurt! But several houses got washed out to sea, and it's going to take a long time to make good the damage."

"Got it," Hans said. He had shut his eyes and was rocking back and forth on his heels. "They were prepared to put up with any sort of suffering so long as it was under their control. They wanted to be victims of their own decisions. Hence the ritual of whipping and sometimes killing. But when the suffering came from beyond their sphere of influence, it reduced them to the condition of mindless animals—that's by definition, in terms of their creed. Coupled with the fact that no matter how confident Yard might sound, he could never be sure that Long had not voluntarily abandoned Azrael and its ideals. Neat! Oh, very neat! A good tight snare, better than the one I invented!"

"You keep talking about Azrael in the past," Captain Inkoos said, sounding puzzled. "Past tense, I mean."

"That's where it belongs," said Alida immediately. "Along with all the other human societies so terrified by the fragility of their own uniqueness that they had to brand their members by deforming them. Your ancestors must have done the same, I guess; I'm sure mine did."

"Well, sure they did. But I never expected anything like that to crop up in the here-and-now." Captain Inkoos licked her broad lips. "And I still don't see why setting off one explosion did more to change their minds than Hans could by all his reasoning."

"Ah, that's what proves they aren't so insane as to be past hope," Hans stated promptly. "It merely showed them there are some events which could, in their own terms of reference, reduce them to a condition they affected to despise. That's to say, they would have no control over how and when they died. That's what has convinced me it was worth my while to risk trying to save them. I didn't admit that was what was in my mind, and it's as well. Because in the upshot someone had to come along and save me!" He turned to Alida. "I hope you realise you saved not only my life but my sanity?"

"And I hope," she returned gravely, "that you remember how to show gratitude. But it isn't really to me that you owe a debt, you know."

"But it was because of you that—"

She cut him short. "In the ultimate analysis, we owe it all to Jorgen."

"What?"

"Lorenzo said categorically that had it not been for having Jorgen in his care, he might not have realised what was wrong with Lancaster Long."

"What in the whole of space did Jorgen's breakdown have to do with the situation here on Azrael?"

Alida shrugged. She said, "I guess we'll have to go back to Earth to find that out. But on the strength of what I've so far been told, it's a question of putting too great a burden on a single person."

Hans thought for a moment. Then his face lit up.

"Oh! Oh, *yes!* The nobility of Azrael were too frightened to let more than one of their number go to Earth, even though he had a retinue of attendants. But we require that someone in Jorgen's position always travel alone with no more help than can be assured by portable machines, and I denied myself even that, and—and I've given up being a fool, Alida. The pantologist rôle is far too solitary for comfort. I'm going to cling to what I've learned: there will always be a shock you can't prepare for."

"Who needs to be told so?" grumbled Captain Inkoos, and signalled to her attending officers that it was time to withdraw the landing-ramp and head for orbit prior to firing up another Bridge.

XIV

————◆◆————

Humming a cheerful tune, Alida entered her office
. . . and stopped dead in her tracks. Her hand flew to
her throat, as though to beckon words.

"Jorgen!" she said faintly. "I didn't expect to find
you here! How—?"

"Oh, I'm the Director of the System, remember?"
Thorkild said. "All doors in the Bridge Centre open
for me."

He sat before a screen on which were cycling all
the news headlines for the past day or more, and on
another chair, behind him and to one side, sat a slender girl, very young, with dark hair gathered on the
nape of her neck and wide dark frightened eyes.

"This is Nefret," Thorkild said as an afterthought.
"She was in the hospital with me. She tried to escape
from Earth the day Saxena killed himself. I don't suppose you remember. I didn't until accident brought us
together—if you can call anything planned by
Lorenzo accidental. I promised her what she wants,
which is anything that matters, and I imagined I'd
found what I was after because Lancaster Long had so
insulted me. Now I've a mind to turn right around
and go back when she and I came from!"

Alida hesitated; then she rounded her desk and took her normal seat behind it. Secure in a familiar posture, she said, "Do you mean because Azrael changed its collective mind?"

"You know damned well what I mean! I came out of the hospital all set to beat Long and his kinfolk over the head until they agreed with me that what they needed to save them was a Bridge, and found instead that—"

"Wait," Alida said, raising her hand. "You don't already realise that it was because of you—not because of me, not because of Hans, but because of *you*—that the people Long left behind decided to accept a Bridge after all?"

He blinked in confusion. "Me? What did I have to do with it? Any more than those fake Azraelites I saw coming here!"

She leant forward.

"But you were a real one!"

There was a dead pause. At long last, dry-mouthed, Thorkild said, "What in hell do you mean?"

"I mean precisely this." Alida sat back in her chair again. "Because you were so remote from any personal reward for the effort you were investing, you were as inclined as the people of Azrael on their hostile, dull, *boring* planet to assume that life wasn't worth living. That the only thing worth planning for was how to get the hell away from it. But this was the trap Saxena fell into—"

"You think that's what drove him to suicide?" Thorkild cut in.

"Now, I believe it must have been. One can never be sure. But it makes better sense than anything else. Doesn't it? And on top of that, there's something Moses pointed out to me. We don't—I mean people like you and me—risk having children."

"If it weren't for my work!" Thorkild exclaimed. "I've always wanted to be a parent—"

"Enough to sacrifice twenty or more years of your life to raising them in the ideal circumstances you or I can envisage?"

She paused long enough for the implications to sink in, then resumed.

"We actually don't. And above all pantologists don't, who can envisage the idea better than anybody. We rely on replacements for ourselves emerging from the gene-pool. This is a reflection of what happened on Azrael, sort of. There was a caste-system dependent on thinking alike. They've been branding their peers and successors—"

"Got it!" Thorkild broke in. "Don't spell out the rest. I know it now. Just tell me what I did to be what you called a real Azraelite!"

"Why, called in question the meaning of existence! What did you think I meant?"

"And lost out in my argument with the rest of us, when I tried to maintain that existence was totally pointless?"

"Mm-hm!" Alida nodded vigorously. "For if it is, we simply don't possess—and never shall possess—the evidence to prove it. Like you, we have to accept that it will be worth enduring life even if we can't copy ourselves. And parents never have been able to do that. The universe forbids it."

A slow smile was creeping across Thorkild's face. He said, "The people on Azrael thought of their children as potential sacrifices."

"Hey!" Alida slapped the top of her desk. "Hans would have been proud of that phrase if he'd got to it before you! It ties in with all the military cultures of Old Earth, and—No, that's for later. Right now, I want to know for certain that you recognise what you did to trigger the solution for us all."

"All?" Thorkild echoed ruefully. "Well, I guess if my example helped Hans, it must indirectly have helped us all . . . I'm not going back into hiding, at any rate. I'm set on finding out what can meet my demands, and Nefret's—that is, what matters."

"I wouldn't want more for myself," Alida said.

"Shall I—?" Thorkild hesitated. "Shall I come back?"

"Yes. Yes please, Jorgen. It won't be long before Hans goes where I have no hope of following him. And I suspect when something similar happens to you . . ." She shook her head and forced a smile.

"Understood," Thorkild said gravely, and rose, offering his hand to Nefret. Who took it docilely and followed him.

"Oh, by the way," Alida called as they were leaving, and they glanced back in the maw of the exit.

"Yes—what?" Thorkild said.

"Right here on top of my priority file is something not for me but for you." Alida indicated the screen, out of sight of them, which was presenting her accumulated messages. "It's from Koriot Angoss. Says he's desperately anxious to have you drop in. But won't say why."

"Sort of confident, isn't he, that I'll make it back to the land of the living?"

"You did," Nefret said loudly and clearly. "Take me with you! That's all I ask! I've been to my Azrael and I didn't like it. Help me find somewhere else—you promised!"

"We all need to find somewhere better than Azrael," Thorkild said.

Perversely, he led her to Angoss's office by the route he had taken on the day the crisis broke, as though to defy omens. Gazing in disbelief down the huge corridors which he exposed to her sight, she whispered, "This is always here? And no one notices it? Why, if I'd known there was something this big hidden behind the walls of the world they made me live in, I'd never have acted the way I did! Thank you so much for showing me!"

She checked him in mid-stride and threw her arm around his neck, crushing her mouth against his.

For a moment he resisted, but only for a moment. Her tongue spoke to his too eloquently without words.

When they had to separate and draw breath, she said against his cheek, "I'm torn apart. I want to be your daughter and your lover. I don't know what my nature is, you see. I'm only hoping that you may have found out what yours is after all you've been through. After all, you did start looking later than I had to. Make me a person, please!"

"I'm not sure I've found out more than you have," Thorkild muttered, and urged her onward.

The door named after Koriot Angoss swung open. He and Maida Wenge were stooping over a sort of cage, wherein was movement. Thorkild gave a wild shout.

"Shall I never find you at work? What have you there—something to remind you of the fauna back home?"

Angoss stared at him. "I was sure you would recover," he said after a pause. "So I sent for something that ought to help with convalescence. Look!"

He held out the cage. Thorkild saw the thing moving inside was a snake. All at once he was calm.

"I've been out of touch," he said. "But I deduce that Long gave Rungley such a boost that he's still causing trouble. Am I right?"

"As of now, sure you are," said Angoss. "In fact the Azrael Society has been making a big thing about snake-handling and a gang of fools have gone to their repose. But not as of tomorrow, I promise you."

"How do you mean?"

"This snake here is poisonous in a big, big way. Already by making them accept the Bridge Mr Hans Demetrios has seen off the crazy folk at Azrael. Some people don't know what's good for them. It makes me shamed that we have a few on Riger's as bad as Lancaster Long. So here you see I had our chemists develop an additive for snake-venom which attacks this enzyme Rungley trusts in. Any other snake he can ignore, but not this. Mine will make him very sick, I tell you. Are you pleased?"

The universe seemed to grind to a halt. Then light broke in on Thorkild's mind brighter than the sun.

Insoluble problem: a snake-handler immune to venom. Answer: a snake he's not immune to.

Insoluble problem: a planetful of people who reject the overtures every other human world has found attractive. Answer: make an overture so nasty that anything else will seem attractive by contrast.

Insoluble problem: your predecessor died rather than face the demands of the job you hold. Answer: instead of falling in love with the most mature, competent and insightful woman around, which is what he did, you fall for a fellow patient in a mental asylum, who is actually looking for a father.

Insoluble problem: lack of incentive to go on living. Answer: impossibility of finding an incentive to abolish life. Even the master-minds of Azrael hadn't managed that. Even under the goading and provocation of Hans Demetrios, who could have needled them into it if anybody could, they didn't make it.

There was still the universe. And there were still people prepared to endure the torment of inhabiting it. It figured. In a cockeyed, roundabout, upside-down sort of way, it figured.

"Human beings aren't very logical creatures, are they?" Thorkild said aloud.

Angoss blinked. "Never have been," he said. "Not to my knowledge. Leave that to computers, I say. Got better things to do."

Thorkild nodded slowly. "I think I have, too. I was all set to envy Alida, you know, because she was so damned smart—and, you know, she really *is*, because at least once she outsmarted a pantologist, and that's Hans, and he's bound to go way out yonder where none of us can follow, and even Jacob Chen got killed on the way there . . . But it doesn't matter! No more than anything else does! I have my job to do, because machines said I was fit for it, and they said the same to Moses van Heemskirk, and they said it to Minister Shrigg, and sometimes I think they're marvellous, and sometimes I think they must be as crazy as the Azrae-lites, and . . ." He swallowed hard. "And because it's impossible for one person to be sure about everything, the man I most admire of all the people I have ever met is Hans Demetrios, who says he owes a debt to me, but whom I owe a debt to, far bigger and impossible to repay. He faced something I could never face: he took the risk of being convinced that he was wrong. I only decided I'd been beaten. That was so trivial I changed my mind. Now I believe I can't be."

"I'm not sure I followed what you were saying," Nefret whispered. "But it sounded good." She advanced on the snake, seeming fascinated. "What are you going to do with—with this?"

"Permit it to be true to its nature," Thorkild said. "In order to straighten out a man who isn't being true to his. Which is about as much as any snake has ever done."

"The Garden of Eden?" said Angoss in a doubtful voice. "There was one there, they told me."

"It didn't do any more," said Thorkild. "Nothing can, and nothing ever will."

Don't miss any of these SF winners:

By JOHN BRUNNER